M000219489

THE DEPTHS

Praise for *The Depths*

A sensational book—an absolute fever blister of a thriller that manages also to be a fine, nearly heartbreaking character study. I'll be recommending it all year.

> – Timothy Hallinan, author of the Poke Rafferty and Junior Bender novels

Kjeldsen's short novel moves at a blistering pace, putting Marah through one ordeal after another . . . This tense, haunting tale gives readers front-row seats to the protagonist's torment.

> – *Kirkus Reviews*

The Depths is a wonderful novel: lyrical, yet still relentless and utterly engrossing. Few writers have explored the ragged fault line where western sensibilities struggle with the enigmas of Asia, and absolutely no one has done it better than this.

> – Jake Needham, author of the Jack Shepherd and Inspector Samuel Tay novels

A dark, engaging, and contemplative thriller.

> – *Foreword Reviews*

Kirk Kjeldsen's latest is a tight, spare tale of a romantic getaway gone horribly wrong. As the punishing snare of the jungle tightens around husband and wife, Marah and Eden will learn that the worst dangers arise from inside— as does the only real means to survive.

> – Jenny Milchman, author of *Cover of Snow* and *Wicked River*

A gut-punch of a thriller, wickedly paced and beautifully rendered.

> – Peter Swanson, author of *Her Every Fear* and *The Kind Worth Killing*

A holiday gone wrong, and every traveler's worst nightmare when a couple is kidnapped while on vacation in Malaysia. Kirk Kjeldsen delivers in *The Depths* — a tense and action-packed story that seems built for the big screen. Breathless suspense!

> – Kimberly Belle, author of *The Marriage Lie* and *Three Days Missing*

With strong prose and stunning imagery, *The Depths* takes the thriller genre to the next level . . . a pleasurable read, immensely satisfying in its suspense.

> – *IndieReader*

Kirk Kjeldsen's latest is a totally engrossing kidnapping story that careens through the wilds of Malaysia to a violent, twisty, satisfying conclusion. Genuinely horrifying, yet a fun read.

> – Alan Hruska, author of *Pardon the Ravens*, *Wrong Man Running*, and *It Happened at Two in the Morning*

Kjeldsen drops us into the darkest abyss — that expanding chasm between an estranged husband and wife, powerless to protect one another, or connect, in the most excruciating of circumstances. Unflinching and raw in its prose, *The Depths* takes 'til death do us part to its most terrifying fathomage . . . and never resurfaces.

> – Clay McLeod Chapman, author of *Miss Corpus* and *Rest Area*

Praise for *Land of Hidden Fires*

Kjeldsen tells a small-scale tale about Norwegian resistance to the Nazis in this work that should appeal to historical thriller fans . . . His descriptive prose does a fine job of conveying the breathtaking scenery of the wintry Norwegian mountains.

– Publishers Weekly

Land of Hidden Fires is a compelling testament to the dangers, and necessity, of resistance. Kjeldsen writes about the quiet horrors of life in wartime with clear-eyed humanity and grace.

– Colin Winnette, author of *Haints Stay*

Despite the high drama and action-driven hunt, the story remains at its core a quiet one, focused on the well-developed, internal struggles of the characters and with the careful, evocative use of language . . . Kjeldsen's writing benefits from a deep underlying knowledge, not only of World War II ranks and weaponry—though history buffs should appreciate the details—but also of farming techniques, the hazards of a winter trek through Scandinavian woods, and animal behavior . . . A quiet and introspective novel of wartime adventure.

– Kirkus Reviews

A fine wartime tale of survival and resistance, told with clean, compelling prose. The tough and resourceful Kari will linger in your memory, and the evocative setting will leave you shivering beneath the sheets.

– Dan Fesperman, author of *The Letter Writer*

Kirk Kjeldsen's non-fiction turned novel is a fitting memorial to heroes whose lights shine in dark times . . .

The novel is full of suspense and drama, and the author succeeds in casting light on a very dark period of Norway's history.

– The Norwegian American

As much a love letter to his family's homeland as it is a thrilling adventure of World War II, Kirk Kjeldsen's *Land of Hidden Fires* shows that underneath Norway's snow and ice lies a burning heart.

– Alan Gratz, author of Prisoner B-3087
and Projekt 1065

Creating tension is just one of Kjeldsen's talents. Another is utterly capturing the mindset of a sheltered teenage girl who is falling in love with her rescued (and indifferent) pilot, imagining herself going to America with him. And third, but far from last, is Kjeldsen's writing. He has masterfully set a story, fraught throughout with danger, against an icy, white, virtually silent tableau — a story that will stay with you long after you've finished it.

– New Jersey Star-Ledger

Praise for *Tomorrow City*

A tight, tense crime novel about a stranger in a strange land trying to outrun the ghosts of his past. Kirk Kjeldsen's Shanghai is a terrifically fresh and evocative setting, and the action jumps off the page.

– Lou Berney, author of Whiplash River, Gutshot Straight, and The Long and Faraway Gone

Kjeldsen creates drama and danger with ease, and the events that follow are riveting. This is a literary thriller in the best sense of the term . . . His smart, penetrating story is not to be missed.

– New Jersey Star-Ledger

Tomorrow City is a vicious little tale of men and violence and the sucking black hole of the past. A coiled and sleek throwback noir, best read in one shot. More please.
– Elwood Reid, author of *If I Don't Six, Midnight Sun,*
and *D.B.*

Kirk Kjeldsen has written a one-sitting novel with an ex-con protagonist you'll eagerly follow across the globe as he tries to shake his past. *Tomorrow City* is as exciting as it is smart as it is heartbreaking.
– Michael Kardos, author of *The Three Day Affair* and
Before He Finds Her

Tomorrow City unfolds with grace and power, building to a cinematic climax that reverberates long after you've finished reading. This is thriller writing at its finest. Kjeldsen is one to watch.
– Carlo Bernard, writer of *The Great Raid* and
executive producer/co-creator of *Narcos*

Tomorrow City is darn near a perfect book — fierce, intelligent, gritty, and absolutely convincing. You can certainly count me as a fan of Kirk Kjeldsen.
– Martin Clark, author of *The Jezebel Remedy*, *The Legal
Limit*, and *The Many Aspects of Mobile Home Living*

With spare but riveting prose — and the rare ability to elicit the reader's sympathy for a criminal — Kjeldsen has produced a thriller with plenty of the requisite shocks, a fully drawn protagonist, and a serious look at issues of justice and morality.
– Richmond Times-Dispatch

In *Tomorrow City*, the dark past of a former American criminal catches up with him in the chaotic streets of Shanghai. Exciting action in an exotic setting. Read. You'll enjoy.

– Tom Epperson, author of The Kind One and Sailor

I had a twofold pleasure in reading Kjeldsen's debut. As a writer, I admired his skill at evoking a sense of place and his uncommon ability to evoke sympathy for a criminal. But the real payoff came as a reader: *Tomorrow City* is *such a cracking good story.*

– Leighton Gage, author of Perfect Hatred, Blood of the Wicked, and Every Bitter Thing

Kirk Kjeldsen jabs a needle into the soft spot where nightmares intersect with real life and injects a steady dose of speed. *Tomorrow City* is a relentless, surprising and harrowing tour of the fascinating underside of Shanghai.

– David Rich, author of Caravan of Thieves and Middle Man

Also by Kirk Kjeldsen

TOMORROW CITY
LAND OF HIDDEN FIRES

THE DEPTHS

A novel
Kirk Kjeldsen

Grenzland Press

The Depths
By Kirk Kjeldsen
Published by Grenzland Press
Copyright © 2018 Kirk Kjeldsen
ISBN-13: 978-0-9984657-3-9
eBook ISBN: 978-0-9984657-4-6

www.grenzlandpress.com

Cover design: Rafael Andres
Author photograph: SoMi Photographie

for my mother

"Consider the subtleness of the sea; how its most dreaded creatures glide under water, unapparent for the most part, and treacherously hidden beneath the loveliest tints of azure. . . . Consider all this; and then turn to this green, gentle, and most docile earth; consider them both, the sea and the land; and do you not find a strange analogy to something in yourself?"

— Herman Melville, *Moby-Dick; or, The Whale*

CHAPTER ONE

The fog appeared after they passed over Mount Kinabalu.
At first, it looked like a tuft of dirty cotton. Then it looked
like a spreading ink stain. Before long, it filled the horizon.
It rolled over them like a slow, gray wave, swallowing
them whole.

Marah Lenaerts sat in seat 7F, staring out the
window. It seemed as if she were looking into her own
soul, somehow; since her third miscarriage, she'd felt like
she'd been drowning in a thick, gray sludge. At the advice
of a colleague, she'd begun counselling at one of
Shanghai's international hospitals, but it hadn't helped.
The psychiatrist had recommended an antidepressant to

her, but she'd declined, ashamed at seeking help in the first place and worried it might hinder her chances of getting pregnant again.

After a moment, the sound of her husband's voice snapped her from her daydreaming.

"Prawn or crab?" he asked.

She turned to see Eden returning to his seat, holding two bags of Malaysian junk food. Despite his expensive haircut and Hugo Boss shirt, his blue-collar Belgian upbringing shone through in his clipped speech and brusque manner.

"I asked what the locals like," he said, his slight cleft lip bisecting the top of his grin.

"Prawn, I guess," she said.

"Smart choice."

He gave her the prawn crackers. Then he tore into the crab chips, stuffing a handful into his mouth. Marah stared at the cartoon shrimp on her bag; even in animated form, it reminded her of a fetus, curled up and undeveloped. *God,* she thought to herself, *why does everything remind me of babies?*

"These movies are shit," said Eden, scrolling through the options on the seatback screen in front of them before selecting an action film.

Marah looked over at him with her wide, glassy eyes. There was so much she wanted to say, but she was afraid that if she opened her mouth, it would all come crashing out like the waters from a burst dam and carry him away. Instead, as she'd done so often in recent months, she said nothing and glanced back out the window, where hazy shapes merged and broke apart in the fog. She saw a cell splitting into two, and then imagined a grenade exploding.

Then she saw a school of koi fighting over some bread and, finally, a misshapen skull.

Tawau's airport stood in a clear-cut section of jungle situated near the Jalan Utara access road. A few short- and medium-range jets taxied toward its sole runway, awaiting clearance for takeoff.

Marah waited for their luggage at one of the airport's three baggage claims while Eden got a cart. Throngs of Chinese and Malay passengers waited with her, talking and checking their smartphones. Despite the sweltering heat, most of the Malay women wore long-sleeved shirts and hijabs, while the men were dressed in short-sleeved shirts and slacks. An older man wearing a purple *songkok* stared at Marah's shorts and bare shoulders; she looked away, only to see another man glaring at her.

Growing uncomfortable, Marah took a sweater from her backpack and pulled it on. A baby cried out nearby, its reedy wail piercing through the noise. Marah turned to look, noticing that the baby's teenaged parents were practically children themselves. It didn't seem fair, somehow — children having children — whereas she'd had two D&C procedures, met with Shanghai's top fertility experts, and tried a number of expensive diets and drugs, but still couldn't manage to carry a child into the second trimester. Feeling a bout of sadness coming on, she took out her cell and scrolled through her emails; there were a few from her students as well as one from her mother, Carolyn, who'd sent photos of the turning leaves in northwestern New Jersey, where she'd been living for the past fifteen years with Marah's wealthy stepfather, Tom. Marah sent her mother a quick reply — "Beautiful! xoxo" — before responding to her students' emails. Most of them were wealthy Chinese teens with self-chosen Western names like Mars, Rolex, and Ice, studying English in preparation for life at American universities. Teaching ESL was far from where she'd thought she'd end up after graduating from NYU with a double major in art history and English. Marrying a Belgian was far from what she'd envisioned as well, but she'd met Eden at a time she'd needed an escape from the life that she was heading toward. He was different than the guys she'd dated in college, more confident and exotic, yet in a safe way (he was from Belgium, after all, and not Bolivia or Baghdad).

When he'd gotten a job offer in Singapore, she'd gladly left her publishing job to go along with him; Asia seemed like the future, whereas the publishing industry seemed like it was on its last legs. Eden's two-year assignment at HSBC's trading desk in Singapore had become a four-year assignment when a promotion brought them to Hong Kong, though, and when he'd left that for a position with Credit Suisse in Shanghai, she'd taken up teaching English at the Happy Bridge International School in Shanghai's Min Hang district. It wasn't exactly what she'd planned, but life had had its way of making its own plans, a fact made painfully clear to her when her father had succumbed to cancer at the age of forty-one.

The conveyor belt soon whirred to life, and the bags slowly began to emerge. Marah put away her cell phone and looked for their luggage, spotting their roller duffel bags first, which they used to transport their diving gear. Then she saw Eden's suitcase, a leather-trimmed Globe-Trotter he'd bought a couple of years ago, before the market had tanked. She reached for one of the duffel bags, but before she could grab it, Eden approached and lifted it off the belt.

"I got it, babe," he said. She watched as he put their luggage on a rusty cart, the knotty muscles of his arms moving like small animals beneath his skin. She felt a warmth slowly beginning to unfurl inside of her, then

began to grow self-conscious again and tugged her
sweater down over the small bulge left by her
pregnancies.

"You really think we should be doing this?" she
asked.

"Come on," he said. "We need a break."

"We could've gone to the States."

"Visiting family isn't vacation, Mar."

"I know, but still—"

"Don't worry," he said, interrupting her. "It's gonna
be great. I promise."

He grinned again, and she forced a smile back. The
vacation had been his idea; they were individually and
collectively out of sorts, and they'd needed some time off,
he'd argued. She'd reluctantly agreed—not because she'd
wanted to go, but because she felt she'd needed to go.
Eden had become distant since her third miscarriage, and
she felt like she was losing him somehow, to work, to his
hobbies, or worse—to someone else. He'd always been
faithful to her, or if he hadn't been, he'd at least been
discreet, unlike her sister's husband, Brent, a hedge fund
manager who openly chased anything in a miniskirt. Eden
had been pulling away recently, though, talking less to her
in the morning while they got ready for work, making
fewer dinner reservations for them, and going more often
and later to the gym. He touched her less, and he made

less eye contact with her. Every time his cell phone vibrated at night or he returned home late from work, the engines of panic and doubt whirred to life in her mind.

Eden finished loading their luggage onto the cart and they started for the exit, where two young Malay soldiers armed with machine guns stood guard. Marah felt her mouth go dry, one of the precursors to the panic attacks she'd been having since her last miscarriage. In baggy navy uniforms two sizes too big for them, the soldiers hardly looked old enough to shave, let alone carry automatic weapons. Marah imagined them accidentally firing their guns, barely hanging on to them as they randomly sprayed bullets into the crowd. On their way past, though, the soldiers didn't even glance at them, more interested in a group of teenage girls milling about nearby.

They hit a wall of humidity as they stepped outside the terminal, a harbinger of the approaching monsoon rains. It was late September, off-season for tourists and one of the hottest times of the year in Sabah. Overhead, the sky was the color of setting concrete, thickened with the haze from the annual field clearance fires in nearby Indonesia. It reminded Marah of the Philippines, Vietnam, and some of the other countries they'd visited, though there was a palpable feeling in the air, some heavy sort of electricity that reminded her of the way it felt just before a storm.

After Eden got money from the ATM, he headed over to a vendor's stall.

"Thirsty?" he asked, grabbing a bottled water from a refrigerated case.

Marah nodded, though what she really wanted was a vodka tonic, or at least a cold beer. Eden grabbed a second bottled water and paid the Pakistani vendor with some of the colorful ringgits he'd just gotten from the ATM. After he got his change, he gave one of the waters to Marah. Then he opened the other for himself and drank it in a gulp.

They crossed the parking lot and approached the shuttle bus to Semporna, where they'd planned to meet Hish, a local whose beachfront property Eden had arranged to rent. Eden preferred staying at out-of-the-way villas and guesthouses when they vacationed; they had character, he believed, and authenticity, unlike the large resorts and chains that didn't vary from city to city or even country to country. In Thailand, they'd stayed at an open-air bungalow fifteen minutes' drive from Hua Hin, and in the Philippines, when the market was bullish and Eden was making a fortune, they'd stayed on a private island near Busuanga. The uncertainty of the places he'd find and the people he'd rent them from always made Marah uneasy, but they were far more interesting and memorable than the generic Marriotts or Hiltons she would've settled for.

Eden loaded their luggage and gear into the shuttle bus's baggage hold. Then they boarded the bus, entering a cloud of diesel fuel, curry paste, and sweat. The passengers were mostly Malay, Chinese, and Indian, and their possessions spilled from their bags and seats and into the aisles. The only other Westerner aboard was a middle-aged German backpacker with a much younger Thai girlfriend.

They approached a pair of empty seats near the back and sat down, and a moment later, the driver boarded the bus and pulled out of the station. While Eden checked emails on his cell, Marah stared out the window at the vast palm oil plantations as they scrolled by. There wasn't much else to see along the pocked, two-lane road from Tawau to Semporna, other than a few small ramshackle villages, a windy, tea-brown river, and a crumbling Chinese cemetery.

Her thoughts soon began to drift again, back to Shanghai, to work, and before long, to her ovulation cycle. She wondered if she'd been timing things wrong, then wondered if she was taking the wrong fertility medications, or not enough of them. Not wanting to sink back into the quicksand of despair, she tried to think of something to say to Eden, some benign conversation starter.

By the time she finally did, though, she looked over and discovered that he'd fallen asleep.

A traffic jam clogged the center of Semporna. Scores of honking *kereta sapu* and yellow vans offered rides to the arriving tourists, their drivers shouting offers in a slurry of English and Malay.

Marah turned off the Sharon Van Etten album she'd been listening to as they pulled into the station, and Eden woke as the bus lurched to a shuddering halt. They got off the bus and got their luggage from the hold, then made their way toward the center of town. Local teens loitered outside the Milimewa supermarket, laughing and sharing Texas 5 cigarettes, while a group of Muslim men congregated outside a whitewashed mosque.

After buying some groceries at the Milimewa, they headed toward a roundabout where Eden had agreed to meet Hish. Marah looked toward the seafront, where dozens of diving outfitters and tour operators with hand-painted signs clustered around a group of jetties. In the distance, the emerging moon shone above the Celebes; it reminded Marah of a communion wafer somehow, even though she hadn't been to church since she was a child.

They soon passed a malnourished young mother and her three children sitting on a flattened cardboard box.

The children looked tired and hungry, and the youngest was crying and rubbing his dirty, bloodshot eyes. Something ached inside Marah, and she turned to Eden.

"Give me some money," she said.

"What for?" he asked.

"Come on," she said. "Just give me some money."

Eden handed Marah some ringgits, which she immediately gave to the woman.

"Softie," said Eden.

Marah shoved him, grinning, and he shook his head but couldn't help but laugh. As they walked off, she reached for his hand, and he took her hand in his. His palm was larger than hers, and his calloused skin felt like old leather. She always felt safe and protected in his grip, the same way she'd felt holding her father's hand as a girl.

They soon reached a roundabout with three giant concrete prawns in its center. No one was there, though, other than a toothless beggar sleeping on a bench.

"You sure this is where we're supposed to meet him?" asked Marah.

Eden nodded. "He said to meet by the giant shrimp. How many can there be?"

Marah glanced around at their surroundings as Eden dialled a number on his cell. She noticed a trio of rough-looking locals watching them from a *mamak* stall across the way. They wore long shorts and stained tank tops, and their thin, muscular arms looked like machetes. One of the men wore a baseball cap and had long, ratty hair and a sparse beard. *Bunga terung, ukir rekong,* and other tribal tattoos covered the torso and arms of another, and the third had a long, puckered scar running down the side of his face.

She turned back to Eden. "Well?" she asked.

"He's not answering," he said.

Marah glanced back at the young men as Eden hung up and dialled again, and a knot began to form in her stomach. She looked up the street, toward the Semporna seafront, where she saw the six-story Seafest Hotel, the largest and most modern-looking building in town. It looked completely out of place with its surroundings, like it had been airlifted in from Omaha; it also looked completely familiar and safe. Marah imagined herself sitting in a hot tub in one of the Seafest's suites, blissed out while reading some trashy magazine.

"Maybe we should stay there," she said, practically feeling the pulsating jets of the hot tub drumming against her skin.

Before Eden could reply, they heard a voice behind them.

"Mr. Lenaerts?"

They turned to see a young local in baggy jeans and a Cleveland Cavaliers T-shirt, followed by a much-older man wearing a more traditional black *songkok* and *baju melayu*. The young local smiled wide, revealing a cemetery of bright, crooked teeth.

"Welcome to Semporna," he said.

CHAPTER TWO

They rode off in Hish's rusty Proton Saga. The car reeked of stale *nasi lemak*, cheap deodorant, and cigarette smoke. Hish drove, and his grandfather Irfan sat next to him in the passenger's seat, staring blankly at the road ahead. Neither wore a seat belt. MIO, Reef Aljafri, and other Malay hip-hop CDs filled a sleeve on the overhead visor, but Hish left the stereo off, tapping along on the steering wheel to some phantom beat.

Marah and Eden sat in back with their knees bunched up and their smaller pieces of baggage on their laps. Eden checked emails on his cell again while Marah stared at the road ahead of them. Every time Hish jerked the manual transmission up or a down a gear, her stomach roiled.

"This your first time to Malaysia?" asked Hish.

Eden shook his head without looking up from his cell. "We live in Shanghai," he said.

"American?"

Marah hesitated, uncomfortable.

"She is," said Eden, again replying without glancing up.

A look of concern flashed across Marah's face, but Hish spoke before she could reply.

"It's cool," he said. "I love America. Dr. Dre's the shit."

Marah forced a smile before looking out the window. They were already at the outskirts of town, and the starry sky had turned a darker shade of purple-black, devoid of Semporna's light pollution. To their right, down by the ocean, a myriad of rickety stilt villages and houseboats covered the waterfront. Small cooking fires burned on a few of the houseboats, lighting up the water like floating candles.

"Those people live on boats?" asked Marah.

Hish nodded. "Sea gypsies," he said.

She watched as a few scruffy Bajau men passed around a bottle, and Hish again noted her concern.

"Don't worry," said Hish. "They don't mess with tourists."

They eventually left the road from Semporna to Kunak and took a windy dirt trail that curved through the mengaris-choked jungle. Hish swerved the small car around a minefield of potholes left by the endless monsoon rains; Marah felt the burn of stomach acid at the back of her throat and stifled the urge to vomit. Eden finally put away his cell phone and gazed out at their surroundings, as wide-eyed as a child in a toy store. They soon emerged from the jungle, and as the dirt trail straightened out before them, they spotted a two-story villa in the distance, surrounded by a high concrete wall.

Next to the villa, a thin pathway led to a trash-strewn beach where a weather-worn boat gently bumped against a pier.

Marah looked over the villa as Hish unloaded their bags from the trunk. With teak accents and a fresh coat of paint, it was much nicer than the run-down longhouse she was expecting. Noting her surprise, Eden grinned.

"Told you," he said.

Hish spoke before Marah could reply.

"Lemme show you around," he said.

Irfan stayed by the car while Marah and Eden followed Hish toward the villa. A huntsman spider scuttled by before them, chasing a small lizard. Marah's wind vanished as if she'd been punched in the gut.

"Don't worry," said Hish. "Those ones aren't poisonous."

What do you mean, those ones? she wondered, her heartbeat accelerating. Envisioning scores of spiders crawling all over her, black and orange and big and small, she felt her throat constricting and felt like she was sucking for air through a straw. Hish unlocked the door and went inside, and Marah followed, closing her eyes and taking a deep, slow breath through her nostrils, a technique the counsellor had recommended to her for dealing with anxiety attacks. An image of herself back at the Seafest's pool with a Blue Hawaii at her side popped into her mind, but she pushed it from her thoughts, knowing that it wouldn't help. She slowly counted in her head until the feeling began to pass, and before long, her airways slowly reopened.

Hish showed them around the villa. With granite countertops and gleaming appliances, the kitchen was better furnished than their kitchen in Shanghai, and the handmade furniture in the living room was an upgrade over their own Pottery Barn tables and chairs. If it weren't for the candy-colored gecko roaming the ceiling, Marah felt like she was almost back in a city. Almost.

They went into the kitchen, where a window looked out onto the inky sea.

"The dishwasher don't work so good, but the microwave's new," said Hish. "Whatever you do, don't drink the water from the tap, all right?"

Marah glanced around, feeling a chill run up her spine when she saw some sort of orangutan-demon mask on a wall. The face looked angry and malevolent, like one of the ape generals from the *Planet of the Apes* films her father had taken her to when she was a girl. She closed her eyes and counted to herself again in her head, waiting for the feeling to pass. They followed Hish upstairs next, where Hish showed them a bedroom with a queen-sized bed draped with insect netting. Another mask hung on a wall, of a bearded, dreadlocked hunter; with empty eyes and a garish, blood-smeared grin, it reminded Marah of a zombie.

"If the bugs get bad, just chuck another net over the bed," said Hish, pointing to a pile of folded nets atop a dresser.

They continued through the villa and finished up on a veranda behind the house. Irfan was there, staring at the gently rolling waves as they lapped against the pier; a pair of rusty, one-speed bicycles leaned against the veranda's railing.

"There's plenty of fresh towels in the closet," said Hish. "If you need more, just hit me up."

He offered them the keys.

"You know how to operate an outboard?" he asked.

Eden nodded, and Irfan grumbled something in Malay.

"What'd he say?" asked Marah.

"Nothing," said Hish.

Irfan grumbled again, looking directly at Marah, and the angry look in his eyes made her skin crawl.

"Why's he so upset, then?" she asked.

"He just thinks women should be covered," said Hish. "You know, with the hijab."

Before Marah could reply, Irfan spoke again, but Hish cut him off. Irfan muttered something and waved his hand before walking off toward the car, and Hish turned back to Marah and Eden.

"You sure you don't want to book my cousin Ali for a dive?" he asked. "I could hook you up."

Eden spoke before Marah could.

"That's all right," he said.

"You change your mind, his card's on the refrigerator. Need anything else, just gimme a call."

Eden nodded, and Hish walked back to the car and got in. Marah watched uncomfortably as Hish turned the car around and drove it back up the dirt road. Then she looked at the jungle all around them.

Somewhere in the distance, a hornbill cried out through the darkness. It sounded like a woman laughing.

CHAPTER THREE

Marah unpacked their groceries in the kitchen. Eden stood at the dining room table, a jumble of open diving maps before him.

"This place is unbelievable," he said.

After she put away all the peanut butter, ramen noodles, and jackfruit they'd bought, she took out the bottle of vodka she'd gotten at the Shanghai airport's duty-free shop and opened it. Then she poured herself a drink and took a long swig.

"You know what Jacques Cousteau said about it?" he asked.

"'Now we have found again an untouched piece of

art,'" she said in a bad accent that sounded more German than French.

"I already told you that?"

"About a hundred times," she said, laughing.

"There's so much here," he said. "Hammerheads and turtles . . . walls that go down hundreds of feet . . ."

Marah envisioned a sheer, underwater cliff and felt her stomach curdle. She took another long pull from her drink.

"I think we should go out past Palau Mantabuan first," said Eden. "Way past all the touristy places. There's supposed to be some amazing caves and a wreck from World War II."

Marah felt her stomach swirling again and felt icy spiders crawling up and down her spine. "Maybe we should reconsider contacting this Ali," she said.

"What for?"

"We've never gone diving out here."

"So?"

"Eden—"

"What are you so afraid of?" he said.

"Nothing."

"Then relax, will you?"

He finished his drink and grabbed his sandals.

"Let's go swimming," he said.

"Now—?"

Before she could finish, he was already gone.

"Hey, wait for me!" she said.

Not wanting to be left alone in the house, she grabbed her sandals and went out the door, then followed Eden down the pathway leading to the ocean, hurrying after him. The air outside was humid and full of insects; birds screeched and cried out in the distance.

"Wait up!" she shouted, her pulse quickening.

They raced down to the waterfront. Eden kicked off his sandals when he reached the sand and walked out into the sea, and after a dozen paces, he turned back to her.

"Come on," he said. "The water's perfect."

She hesitated.

"What are you waiting for?" he said. "Come on!"

She took off her sandals and slowly entered the water. It was the same temperature as the air, making it difficult to tell where the water ended and the air began. The gentle currents pushed and pulled at her, and she felt something brush against an ankle. *Was it seaweed?* she wondered. *Or a jellyfish?* Her stomach roiled. She wasn't enthusiastic about the ocean during the day—she'd gone on day-trip dives with Eden in Thailand and Indonesia, where it had seemed safe, and she'd gone swimming with him whenever they'd gone to the beach, but she'd never go out as far as he did, or past the point where she could no longer stand. At night, the idea of being in the ocean terrified her. She imagined sharks, stingrays, and all sorts of creatures lurking beneath the surface; the dark, silent expansiveness of the ocean took her breath away.

"It's beautiful, isn't it?" said Eden.

"This is crazy," she said, goose bumps spreading across her forearms and stomach.

He slipped his arms around her waist and pulled her close. Then he began kissing her neck.

"Let's do it," he said.

"Out here?"

"Come on," he said, covering her neck with kisses. "Live a little."

She hesitated. He persisted, and after a moment, they stumbled out of the sea and onto the beach, where he pulled off her clothing as they dropped to the sand. Despite her reticence, she felt herself growing aroused, and as she lay back, her right hand automatically reached for his crotch, which had been their routine for the past few years: some light kissing, then a bit of manual stimulation, followed by a quick session of missionary sex. This would generally take place once or twice a week, at most, and always at the end of the day, when they were both exhausted — unless she was ovulating, in which case it would happen more often, but still far less frequently and with far less passion and variety than it did during the first few years of their marriage, when they couldn't keep their hands off each other. Before her hand found his crotch, though, he stopped her.

"Not so fast," he whispered into her ear before moving down toward her stomach. She tried to pull him back up to face her, but he fought against it. She surrendered and went with it, finding herself more aroused by surrendering control. He kissed her belly first. Then he moved to the freckled tops of her thighs, and then the insides of her legs. His fingers circled her sex, and she became wet. He put his tongue to her and darted back and forth, slowly and gently at first and then faster and more forceful. His fingers then joined in, moving in counterpoint to his tongue. She opened like a flower, and within a few minutes, she seized up and came. Then she pulled him up to meet her, and as she kissed him deeply on the mouth, she reached down and guided him inside her.

They made love in the wet sand. She wrapped her legs around his, and with each thrust, he drove deeper and deeper into her, his rhythm ever quickening. She leaned back and lifted her legs, and he buried himself into her as the tide came forward, washing over his feet and eroding the sand beneath them. She closed her eyes, and all her fears and worries fell away, one after the other, like dead leaves falling off a tree, until she was barren, emptied, and there was nothing else but their lovemaking, the infinite sky above them, and the sound of the waves.

Just as she was about to come again, Marah arched her neck and opened her eyes, glancing backward toward the jungle. She felt a chill run down her spine when she saw a pair of silvery eyes staring back at her from the darkness.

CHAPTER FOUR

The jungle came alive at night with a thousand different sounds. There were chattering crow-billed drongos, golden-whiskered barbets that made a loud, trilling call that went *tehoop, tehoop, tehoop,* and bristleheads whose eerie cry sounded like a high-tension wire being hit with a wrench. Frogs belched and croaked in the swamps; giant horned beetles clacked in the trees. Cicadas the size of fists shrieked louder than anything else with their deafening, grinding song. There were screeching gibbons, wailing hornbills, clicking geckos, and the anguished, unrecognizable cries of something that could have been a bird, or a primate, or even some sort of jungle cat. It was enough to drive a person insane, and the noise of it all collectively rose, fell, and rose again, like the tide.

Marah lay in bed, staring at the tribal mask on the wall. Its blood-smeared grin made her stomach turn. It reminded her of a comic book villain, something that lived in the sewers deep beneath a city and only came out at night. The jungle noises somehow seemed to emanate from its mouth, and it sounded to her like hideous laughter.

She glanced over at Eden, who soundly slept next to her. *Bastard*, she thought to herself, shaking her head. She hated him for being able to sleep so easily, but she knew she was just jealous. She wished she were the one lost in some far-off dreamland rather than lying there, anxious and on edge, despite not having slept well in weeks.

She closed her eyes and tried not to think about it. Not thinking about it just made her think about it even more, so she sought a substitute, a strategy that the counsellor had suggested. She thought about work, but that just made her even edgier. Then she thought about the approaching winter break and where they might spend it; she knew that Eden wouldn't want to go back to the States with her, though, and she couldn't blame him, as it meant a sixteen-hour flight, not to mention a week with her boorish stepfather. He'd want to go somewhere exotic again, maybe Cambodia or Myanmar, and thinking about it only made her stomach churn. Eventually, she thought about sex, and for a while, she felt herself finally drifting away, imagining being bound to a four-poster bed in some luxurious Parisian suite. But as her thoughts surrounding sex so often did, she soon found herself worrying about her fertility, and if she'd ever get pregnant again, and if so, if she'd finally be able to carry to term.

After tossing and turning for what felt like hours, Marah finally opened her eyes, and the first thing she spotted was the mask. She got up from bed and slowly approached it; it seemed to be smirking at her. She took it down from the wall and propped it in the far corner of the room, facing away from her, then crawled back into bed and closed her eyes.

Once again, she tried to sleep, but it was impossible; her thoughts kept circling back to the mask.

The sun rose in the east, its light splashing like hot butterfat across the surface of the sea. A few morning birds carved semicircles in the air, wheeling and rising with the breeze.

Marah stood at the sink and looked out the window, watching the end of the sunrise as she dried the previous night's dishes. She'd tried to sleep for another hour, but she had too much on her mind and felt too nervous and on edge. She got up and went downstairs, where she caught up with emails and played a few games of *Candy Crush* on her phone. Then she watched a *CSI* rerun on the villa's flat-screen television until she got bored and went into the kitchen to tidy up.

After she finished cleaning, she left a note for Eden— *Out getting breakfast, be back in a bit, xoxo*. Then she put on her sneakers and went outside. She took one of the old bicycles from where it leaned against the veranda and climbed onto it. She then pedalled off in the direction of town, following the route Hish had taken.

It was slow-going, slogging the one-speed bike through the wet earth of the dirt trail. The jungle was dark even during the day, and biking through it made her think of Ichabod Crane riding his horse through the forest in *The Legend of Sleepy Hollow*, a story that had terrified her as a girl. She tried not to think about it, but just like the night before, she only managed to think about it even more, seeing the Headless Horseman behind every tree and hearing the approaching footfalls of his steed in every sound. She picked up her pace and pedalled as fast as she could until her calves felt like they were being torn away from the bone.

Marah began to pick up speed when she made it to the paved road, and she even got to coast for a while on a downhill stretch. She soon passed the Bajau settlement on the outskirts of town. Most of the men were already gone, along with the *lepa-lepas*, or colorful fishing boats, that had been moored to the stilted houses the night before; groups of copper-skinned women gathered around the cooking fires, doing chores and tending to their young, while reedy children swam and played in the shallows nearby. It seemed far friendlier in the day, full of laughter and life.

Before long, she rode into Semporna just as the first bus of the day from Tawau was arriving. *Kereta sapu* drivers and tour guides swarmed the arriving Australian and European tourists, offering them rides and diving packages. Other Western tourists already staying in Semporna had their breakfasts at the *kopi tiams* and hawker stalls that lined the seafront. Seeing chubby, Crocs-wearing New Zealanders slathered with zinc oxide and wearing fanny packs somehow made the town feel much more familiar to her, and far less foreboding.

She walked past heaps of fresh fish on wooden blocks and small mountains of papaya, prickly rambutan, and breadfruit at the hawker stalls; she heard traffic, bartering, and someone drumming on a *kendang*, and she smelled rotting food, saltwater, and diesel fuel. A group of Muslim women wearing hijabs shopped at the fish markets and food stalls, and some barefoot local children played soccer in a dirt alley. Everything seemed so vibrant and in focus, and Marah finally began to let go and enjoy herself, taking it all in.

She walked her bike past a stinking durian stand, where a vendor used a machete to hack away at the large, prickly fruit. Down by the docks, a number of tourist dive groups prepared to go out with some of the local day-trip operators, and Marah could see many Westerners among them. During the day, Semporna looked much more welcoming and safe than it did at night; Marah didn't see the men from the *mamak* stall anywhere, or anyone else who looked even remotely threatening. It was a vacation paradise, aside from all the litter, and she began to feel much better about being there.

She bought some peanut-filled mochi and coconut *ang ku* at one of the nicer-looking Chinese coffee shops. She bit into one of the mochi, and it tasted heavenly to her, like a hybrid of a warm glazed doughnut and a Reese's Peanut Butter Cup. Noticing her reflection in a nearby window and the small bulge at her midsection, though, she felt guilty and threw the remainder of the mochi into a trashcan. Then she wrapped up the rest of them for Eden and began to push the bicycle back through town.

Marah hopped on the bicycle when she reached the outskirts of town and rode her way back to the house. She challenged herself on the hill leading back to their rental, pedalling as fast as she could. Her chest heaved and her head swam as she inhaled and exhaled in deep, sloppy gulps. She began to feel good about herself again, and optimistic about things.

She soon passed the Bajau settlement and then left the road for the winding dirt trail, and before long, she spotted their rental in the distance, surprised at how quickly she'd made it back. After she parked the bicycle out front, she went inside.

"Eden?" she said, out of breath. "You awake?"

There was no reply. She put down the bag of pastries and headed upstairs.

"Eden?"

There was still no reply. She went into the bedroom and found it empty, and the bathroom was empty, too.

"Honey?"

Hearing no response, she felt the room begin to tilt again, and she felt her heartbeat begin to thud inside her ears. She went over to the window and looked outside, but Eden wasn't out on the veranda, either. She grew queasy, and the world spun.

Marah hurried back downstairs.

"Eden?" she said in a panicked voice.

There was still no reply. She looked in the kitchen, the bathroom, and the living room, but she didn't find him anywhere. She felt her heart race faster, and she began to have difficulty breathing.

"Eden!"

Marah staggered outside and made her way along the trail down to the beach, her heart pounding in her chest. Worst-case scenarios filled her mind; she envisioned Eden drowning and getting attacked by jungle animals. When she reached the waterfront, though, she spotted Eden on the dock, next to the boat. Relief washed over her as she noticed their diving gear — their BCDs, regulators, wetsuits, dive computers, fins, and tanks — spread out on the dock before him.

Eden looked up at her and smiled.

"Ready to go?" he said, grinning.

CHAPTER FIVE

They went out past the Bajau Laut village. The boat's outboard engine was an old two-stroke that barely did twenty knots, but they weren't in a hurry. The weather was perfect, sunny and in the low eighties, and their surroundings were beautiful. The water was so clear that one could see all the way to the ocean floor, and there wasn't a single cloud in the sky.

Eden sat by the stern, manning the tiller. Marah sat near the bow, staring out at the endless expanse of blue before them and letting the wind course through her hair. She felt her worries and concerns diminish more and more the farther that they went. After a while, she turned to face Eden.

"This is amazing," she yelled, shouting over the outboard engine.

"I told you," he shouted back, grinning again.

They went past Bodgaya, Sebangkat, and all the other small islands and sand cays of Tun Sakaran, where a few operator boats were anchored at some of the more popular dive sites. A group of doughy Westerners like the ones Marah had seen in Semporna lolled in the sun and snorkelled in the shallows off tiny Sibuan Island, and though it looked familiar and inviting, she was glad that Eden didn't stop. A returning group of Bajau fisherman soon passed them heading in the other direction, the hulls of their *lepa-lepas* full of sea cucumbers, rabbitfish, and grouper. The fishermen smiled as they went past, their crooked, sun-bleached teeth impossibly white in contrast to their dark skin. Marah couldn't help but smile back, watching after them until their rigs disappeared over the horizon.

She turned to see Eden checking one of his maps and making an adjustment to their course. Then she looked ahead again, her heart hammering with excitement at the endless expanse of blue. Before long, a wisp of green-black appeared on the horizon; it looked like a smudge of ink at first, and then the worn head of a paintbrush. It soon became apparent that it was a cluster of palm trees at the end of a sandy cay about fifty feet long.

"This is it," said Eden, grinning again.

He killed the engine and dropped anchor, then went about preparing their equipment. He wet the BCDs in the ocean and slid them onto the tanks, attached the regulator hoses, opened the submersion pressure gauges' valves, and checked for leaks. After that, he tested the regulators. He grew up helping his father, an Antwerp boilermaker who'd left when Eden was eleven, and he was adept at taking things apart and putting them back together.

Marah watched Eden while he prepared their equipment, growing more and more uncomfortable. The optimism and confidence that had been growing in her began to diminish again, and her thoughts grew fearful and panicky the closer that they got to entering the ocean. She looked down toward the sea and into its depths, imagining all sorts of razor-toothed creatures lurking in its depths. Once Eden was finished preparing their gear, they put on their wetsuits and weight belts, and Eden felt Marah trembling as he zipped her up from behind.

"You nervous?" he asked.

She shook her head, but he didn't believe her.

"Don't be," he said.

He turned around, and she zipped him up. Then he helped her put on her tank and mask before putting on his own.

"You remember the signal for help?" he said.

Marah raised her hand and waved it over her head.

"You remember the signal for 'I just shit myself'?" he asked.

She raised her middle finger, grinning. He smiled, then made a circle with his thumb and forefinger and extended the other three fingers, making the signal for "Are you okay?"

She nodded.

"Stay close," he said.

He pulled on his fins and put up a diver down flag. Then he put one hand over his mask and regulator, held the back of his head with the other hand, and fell backward into the water. Marah pulled on her own fins, took a deep breath, and slowly let it out. Then she followed Eden into the water with a clumsy back roll of her own.

She plunged through the gently cresting waves and into the darkness below. Underwater, gravity slowed to a standstill, and all sound disappeared; it was like being on the dark side of the moon. She felt herself sinking, and she struggled to right herself under the heavy blanket of water. She finally spotted the sun out of the corner of one eye, a shimmering coin of light in the far distance, and she turned herself around until it was directly above her.

Sucking for air through her regulator, she glanced around for Eden, eventually spotting him about a dozen feet away. After their eyes met, he made the signal for "Are you okay?" again. She tapped the top of her head with her elbow extended sideways, signalling that she was. He slowly waved a flat hand up and down a few times, urging her to calm down. Once she did, and began breathing more slowly and deeply, the air bubbles stopped flooding up from her regulator. Eden then beckoned for her to follow him, turning and swimming off toward a long coral reef.

Marah gazed at her surroundings as she swam after Eden. She spotted a boxlike cowfish, puffing its perfectly round mouth like a monkey trying to blow a smoke ring. Then she caught sight of a group of sand launces shooting past, straight as arrows. She saw a tiny sea horse, its dorsal fin fluttering as it swam vertically past. She couldn't help but shake her head, astounded by the variety of life all around her.

They went down to a depth of about fifteen feet. Marah quickly acclimated to being underwater, no longer fighting it or the equipment and enjoying the sensation of being unattached to the world of gravity. They followed the long, endless reef, marvelling over the branching staghorn coral and the huge globes of Faviidae that looked like cartoon Martians' brains. They stared wide-eyed at leafy scorpionfish, moray eels, and colorful dragonets. The water was crystal-clear, and the visibility seemed limitless.

After they finally reached the end of the reef, Eden turned to Marah and gestured for her to go deeper. Before she could signal a reply, he turned and swam off again. She reluctantly followed, inwardly cursing him for going farther and cursing herself for being crazy enough to follow him. They went down to a depth of twenty feet; Eden pointed out some more coral reefs and some small caverns. They saw a mimic octopus, its skin color and texture matching the coral to which it clung. They spotted a slow-moving bumphead parrotfish with the odd profile of a buffalo. They saw tiny boxer crabs and schools of silvery bigeye trevally. Eden turned to Marah again, and she thought she could make out a small smile underneath his mask. She smiled back, and he turned and swam on.

They went deeper, down to twenty-five feet, and then down to thirty. Marah felt her heart swelling up toward her throat. Eden led her to the base of an old oil platform that had collapsed into a jumble of metal rods and broken concrete pillars. There, she saw even more strange and interesting things: spiny devilfish that crawled along the seabed with their fins, soft-bodied nudibranchs in nuclear colors, bug-eyed flying gurnards with semitransparent wings.

Marah peeled off and followed a lightning-shaped pipefish as it headed toward a coral reef. She watched it swim through and around the coral outcroppings,

mesmerized by its electric coloring and its seemingly
effortless motion. She saw one more interesting fish after
another emerge from the seaweed and the stones. It was
like something out of a Disney film or a dream.

After a moment, she glanced back toward the oil
platform, but Eden was nowhere to be seen. She looked
left and then right, panicking when she still couldn't locate
him. Feeling some sort of presence behind her, she turned
around and looked up toward the ocean's surface,
expecting to see him there. Instead of seeing Eden, though,
she saw a young hammerhead shark swimming a dozen
feet above her, moving side to side like a desert snake.

She sucked for air through her regulator, sending a
flood of rippling bubbles toward the surface. She
struggled to back up, thrashing wildly like someone in the
throes of a seizure. Bumping into a reef, she quickly
changed direction. Then she felt something grab her by the
arm. She turned, terrified, expecting to sea a giant octopus
clutching her. Instead, she saw Eden, making the signal for
"Are you okay?" She nodded, then turned and looked
back toward the surface.

The shark was already gone.

They ate a lunch of peanut butter sandwiches, bananas,
and trail mix back on the boat. The hot sun reflected off

the ocean, causing them to squint.

"You should've seen the look on your face," said Eden.

"I wasn't that scared," said Marah.

"You looked like that kid from *Home Alone*, when those robbers got in his house."

"No, I didn't."

"Yeah, you did," he said, laughing.

"How could you even see my face beneath the mask?"

He leaned in and kissed her on the mouth.

"I love you," he said.

Despite being mad at him, she couldn't help but kiss him back. He knew her better than anyone else had ever known her—what she was afraid of, what she would do in any given situation, what she needed even when she didn't know it herself—and she both hated him and loved him for it. She gave him the rest of her sandwich as she often did, and after they finished eating, they drank iced coffee from a thermos they'd brought along. As soon as they were done, they raised the anchor and set out for the site of an old shipwreck Eden had seen on one of his maps.

They arrived near another small cay just after the sun had reached its apex. After they dropped anchor again, Eden rechecked their equipment. Once he was sure that everything was in order, he helped Marah put on hers before putting on his own. Then he raised a diver down flag and entered the water, and Marah tumbled in after him. As soon as they got acclimated and Marah gave him the "I'm okay" signal, they began their descent.

They went down twenty feet, and then twenty-five, and then thirty. The water grew darker the deeper they went, and Marah felt her heart beginning to race again. They soon reached the ocean floor, but there was no sign of any shipwreck. Marah hoped Eden would turn to her and give her the signal to ascend, but she knew better: he looked to the compass on his dive computer, gestured for her to follow him, and then swam off in another direction.

She followed him along an underwater ridge, and they went down to a depth of thirty-five feet, and then forty. A rust-colored stonefish emerged from a group of rocks and swam off, disappearing again as quickly as it had appeared; overhead, a large school of barracuda swam past in a whirlpool-like formation, sending shivers up Marah's spine. Eden changed direction when he spotted a large mound in the distance, but as they approached it, even from afar Marah could see that it was just some stone outcroppings. He continued on, past a tangle of faded plastic bags and laundry detergent bottles caught in an old fishing net. Marah followed, taking in their surroundings; she spotted a golden frogfish covered with bumpy spinules that looked like some sort of coral that had come alive, then watched with awe as a young hawksbill turtle swam past overhead.

Eden changed direction one more time when he noticed a low pile of what looked like rocks off to their right. Marah went after him, and when they reached the pile, they could see that they were likely cannonballs or ballast stones. They continued on, spotting a large weed- and coral-covered piece of pipe jutting up from the sand. Upon closer inspection, they saw some reinforcing rings on the pipe and realized it was a bronze cannon. Eden scraped off some of the coral near the muzzle end of the cannon, uncovering a Portuguese naval shield.

They wandered over the wreck site, tracing a vague outline of the ship in the scattering of eroded frames and hull planks that lay upon the ocean floor. They admired the lead ingots, broken stoneware pitchers, and other remnants from a forgotten era. Eden pointed out a pile of cut bones and gestured to his mouth, and Marah inferred that they must be remains of the ship's provisions. It felt strange and unsettling to be there, like they were disturbing some sort of sacred burial ground. In the vast silence of the ocean, Marah felt like she could hear echoes of the ship's creaking hull, and the unfurling of its sails, and the voices of its long-dead crew.

They turned and began to make their way back to the boat. Eden spotted the entrance to some caverns on their way. He checked his dive computer again to see how much air they had left; satisfied, he beckoned for Marah to follow him. Before she could signal back, he was already swimming off in their direction.

Marah followed Eden, and they soon entered the caverns. Eden turned on his head-mounted lights, and Marah did the same, illuminating the area before them. They swam forward into a large, bell-shaped tunnel, which led into another chamber. At first, Marah felt her chest tightening and her breathing growing shorter, but after a while, something started to happen: she began to forget about her fears, and she became more and more present and in the moment. The farther and deeper they went, the calmer she became. Instead of fighting the adrenalin and fear of the unknown, she began to accept them and even embrace them.

They continued their way through a labyrinth of underground tunnels and chambers until they found the heart of the caverns, where the skeletal remains of some turtles littered the powdery ocean floor. The place had the same sort of timelessness that the wreck site had, but instead of feeling overwhelmed, Marah felt in awe of it and seemed to somehow understand and appreciate her own place within everything. She wandered through the cavern, amazed by its glittering limestone walls and brightly colored ceiling; she stared in awe at all the flashlight fish, spiny cave lobsters, and moray eels residing there. She studied the large, ocean-worn bones of a turtle as if some ancient shaman in the act of divination. She couldn't believe it when Eden approached her and pointed to his dive computer, signalling that it was time for them to head back to the surface.

Marah followed Eden out of the caverns, and they began to make their way back to the boat. She felt buoyant and light, even though they'd been under water for almost an hour. Subjects like her career, her fertility, and their finances began to creep back into her thoughts, but instead of feeling worried, she began to feel optimistic again. *Maybe things would work out after all*, she thought to herself. Maybe she'd get pregnant and carry a baby full-term; maybe they'd grow close again. Maybe the market would bounce back and Eden's career would flourish once more. Anything seemed possible.

They soon approached the boat, and Marah spotted a large shadow next to it as they drew near. At first, she thought it might be a cloud. There was something off about it, though; it was too small, and too angular. Then she realized it was the hull of another vessel, the same width as theirs and about twice as long.

Marah grew nervous and started breathing again in short, quick breaths, fearful it might be the authorities there to punish them for diving without permits. She felt rage, too, rage at Eden for ignoring her pleas to book the dive outfit and rage at herself for obediently going along. She watched as Eden pulled himself up the small ladder at the back of the boat and disappeared on board, then she slowly ascended the ladder a moment after him, expecting to see the Malaysian police in their dark blue uniforms. Instead, her heart nearly stopped when she saw two men with scuffed M16s aboard their boat, struggling to restrain Eden.

Two more armed men in tattered clothes stood in the other boat.

CHAPTER SIX

One of the men grabbed Marah by the arm and yanked
her aboard.

"Get off her—"

Before Eden could finish, the man punched Eden in
the stomach.

"Eden!" she screamed.

The man turned to her, eyes bulging and bloodshot.
She was so close to him that she could see the swaths of
pores across his cheeks.

"Shut up," he said, spitting the words through his
crooked, grimy teeth. She looked toward the man who
held Eden, who had a beard and wore a black kaffiyeh and

dirty maroon track pants.

"What's going on?" she asked.

A longhaired man spoke before Eden could reply; though he wasn't the biggest, he seemed to be the leader of group.

"Where you phones?" he said, speaking English with a glottal, Malay-sounding accent.

Neither Marah nor Eden replied. The man with the bloodshot eyes smacked Eden across the back of the head.

"Talk," he said. "Now!"

Eden nodded toward a canvas beach tote near the bow of their boat.

"They're in there," he said.

The longhaired one said something in fast, choppy, Arabic-sounding Tausug to the fourth member of their group, a scrawny teenager carrying a scuffed FAL 7.62 machine gun and wearing a black do-rag, a baggy Jay-Z T-shirt, and camouflage fatigues two sizes too big. Unlike the others, who appeared to be Moro or Asian with their full, round faces, the teenager was angular and lighter-skinned, and he looked Zamboangueño or Spanish. He rifled through the tote bag, soon finding Marah's and Eden's cell phones, which he brought over to the longhaired man.

"Please," said Eden.

The man with the bloodshot eyes smacked Eden in

the back of the head again.

"I said shut up," he said.

The longhaired man popped the panels off the cell phones, removed the batteries and SIM cards, and tossed them overboard. Marah felt her stomach drop as she watched them sink. She looked toward the cay and thought about jumping overboard and swimming toward it. *But what then?* she wondered. *Even if I somehow made it, what would I possibly do?*

The bearded man pushed Marah toward the longer boat.

"Move," he said.

She stumbled and nearly fell overboard as she stepped onto the flat, wooden speedboat. One of her flippers fell off, and she watched it splash into the water below.

"Go," said the man with the bloodshot eyes, shoving her.

This can't be happening, she thought to herself. *We're on holiday —*

Before she could finish the thought, the man with the bloodshot eyes shoved her again. She stumbled onto the boat, and after Eden joined her, the bearded man followed them aboard.

"Undress," he said.

Marah hesitated.

"You deaf?" said the man with the bloodshot eyes. "Undress. Now."

They began removing their gear. Marah's fingers trembled so much that she couldn't unzip her wetsuit.

"Hurry up," said the man with the bloodshot eyes, shoving her.

Marah looked toward Eden, her eyes pleading and wide. Eden pursed his lips and shook his head, saying nothing; if his look was supposed to reassure her, it didn't. If anything, it did the opposite, only making her even more uncomfortable. Nearby, the longhaired man said something in Tausug to the teenager, and the teenager went through the tote bag again, finding their wallets. He brought them back to the longhaired man, and Marah felt her chest tighten when the longhaired man found Marah's driver's license.

"*Amerikano*," said the longhaired man, showing the license to the others and grinning. He turned back to Marah and Eden.

"America not in charge out here," he said. "I am. Understand?"

"Yeah," said Eden.

The man with the bloodshot eyes grabbed Marah by the arm and shook her.

"Answer him!" he said.

"Y-yes—"

Eden got in the face of the man with the bloodshot eyes.

"Don't touch her!" he said.

The man with the bloodshot eyes jabbed Eden in the gut with the stock of his rifle, cursing in his native tongue, and Eden dropped to a knee, wheezing.

"Eden!"

Marah helped Eden back to his feet, and the longhaired man said something in Tausug to the bearded man. The bearded man then pulled back a plastic tarp, revealing a pair of milk crates full of dirty tools and equipment. He grabbed a Filipino newspaper and a digital camera from one of the crates and brought them to the longhaired man, who shoved the newspaper toward Marah's chest.

"Hold this," he said.

Marah held up the newspaper with a trembling hand. On the bottom of the newspaper, she could see a photo of the smiling Chinese premier, who'd had a meeting that week with the Filipino president and the Malaysian prime minister. She remembered seeing a similar photograph on the cover of one of the Malaysian newspapers that morning, back in Semporna. It suddenly seemed so long ago, even though it had only been a matter of hours.

This isn't happening this isn't happening this isn't happening, she repeated to herself in her head, over and over again, recalling a Radiohead song from her youth. But it was happening, and the more she tried to deny it, the more real it became to her, and the more desperate and crazed her thoughts felt.

The man with the bloodshot eyes shoved Eden toward Marah, pushing them together.

"Smile," said the longhaired man.

Out of reflex, Marah opened her mouth to speak but then hesitated, feeling stupid for being so obedient. The boat bobbed on the sea and she lurched forward, but Eden grabbed her arm, preventing her from falling over. The longhaired man took some photos of them holding the newspaper. Then he said something in Tausug to the man with the shaved head before climbing onto their boat. After the teenager stepped back onto the longer boat, bringing the tote bag with him, the longhaired man untied the boats from one another and pushed off.

"You want to live, do what they say," he said.

Without waiting for a reply, the longhaired man fired up their boat's small outboard engine. Then he turned it around and headed back in the direction of Semporna.

CHAPTER SEVEN

The bearded man pulled Marah's and Eden's shorts and T-shirts from the tote bag and threw them at their feet.

"Put them on," he said.

Marah hesitated.

"You deaf?" shouted the man with the bloodshot eyes. "Put them on! Now!"

The men ravaged Marah with their eyes as she struggled out of her bathing suit. Humiliated, she hurried to pull off her bottoms but ended up getting them caught around an ankle. The more she panicked, the more she struggled, and the men reveled in it, watching it like it was some sort of hideous burlesque.

She finally got the suit off. Then she yanked on her

underwear and her shorts. She fumbled with her bra, unable to fasten the clasp with her trembling hands. After Eden finished dressing, he helped Marah, and she averted her eyes from the leering men. Once Marah and Eden were dressed, the man with the bloodshot eyes barked an order in Tausug to the teenager; with the longhaired man gone, the man with the bloodshot eyes appeared to be in charge.

The teenager slung his FAL 7.62 over his shoulder and dug through one of the milk crates, finding a bag of plastic zip ties. He cuffed Marah's and Eden's wrists behind their backs, pulling the ties so tightly that the plastic teeth dug into their skin.

"Careful," said Eden.

The man with the bloodshot eyes smacked the back of Eden's head again. "Shut up," he said.

While the teenager finished binding them, the other two men found the rest of Marah's and Eden's food. They ripped into it like a pack of jackals tearing into a carcass. Marah envisioned the men ravaging her the way they decimated the food and grew sick to her stomach again. She closed her eyes and pushed the thoughts from her mind, struggling to focus on her breathing. The men didn't save anything for the teenager, and when they were finished eating, they guzzled the rest of Marah's and Eden's coffee before tossing the empty thermos overboard.

The man with the bloodshot eyes barked another order in Tausug to the teenager, and the teenager grabbed the tarp and unfurled it. Then the man with the bloodshot eyes turned back to Marah and Eden.

"Lie down," he said.

Marah hesitated.

"Down," he said, louder. "Now."

Marah and Eden struggled to kneel in the center of the boat. They moved too slowly for the man with the bloodshot eyes, so he kicked Eden in the back. Eden pitched forward, smacking his mouth against the hull with a dull thump.

"Eden—"

Marah lunged to help him, but the man with the bloodshot eyes pushed her down before she could. She hit the hull with her shoulder, sending a sharp bolt of pain down her spine. Then she rolled onto her face, getting a mouthful of dirty seawater. Behind her, the man with the bloodshot eyes barked another order in Tausug to the teenager, and the teenager covered them with the tarp.

The tarp was thin and the sun was strong, so Marah and Eden could still see, though everything was bathed in a cool, blue light. It reminded Marah of a nightlight one of her friends had gotten for her baby daughter, the way that it cast a soft, blue haze over everything. She felt a million miles away from her friend's home, though, and the memory felt like it had taken place a million years before, in another life.

The way they lay, Marah had her back to Eden and couldn't see his face.

"You okay?" asked Eden.

"Where are they taking us?" she said.

"I don't know."

"I'm scared—"

Someone kicked her in the leg, and it felt like she'd been bitten by a dog.

"No talking," said one of the men.

Marah lay in silence for a moment, her calf throbbing. Then she heard the two outboard motors being started, one after the other. They sounded like Harley-Davidsons, rumbling like thunder. Another moment later, the boat began to move.

The light boat had been built for speed, and it was soon flying across the waves. Marah's thoughts went off in a thousand different directions, and her head became a storm of noise. The boat's thin bottom smacked down hard against a trough, and Marah smashed her face into the hull. The coppery tang of blood filled her nostrils and her mouth.

They roasted under the tarp. Even if Marah had wanted to talk, it would have been impossible to hear over the deafening roar of the engines. She rolled to one side with her back still to Eden and struggled to see if she could get an idea of the direction they were heading, but all she could see was the warped side of the boat. The Radiohead song popped into her thoughts again and she tried to shut it out, but the harder she tried to forget it, the louder it only seemed to play.

Time passed slowly, and it was difficult to tell how long they'd been traveling. At one point, Marah felt Eden's fingertips brush against hers, and they tenuously held each other's hands for a moment before the boat smacked down against another trough and separated them. Marah eventually got sick from all the jostling around, and she threw up a bitter mixture of salt water, peanut butter, and blood. She tried not to roll into it as the boat continued to rise and fall, but it kept sloshing and spreading around until she could no longer avoid it.

She thought about shouting to the men, but even if they could have heard her, she knew they wouldn't have cared. She ended up just lying there with her eyes closed, practicing four-count breathing in an effort to avoid hyperventilating. After what felt like a couple of hours, the boat finally started to slow, and the roar of the engines diminished. They heard the voices of the men conversing in Tausug, and a moment later, someone pulled off the tarp.

The teenager yanked Marah to her feet while the

bearded man pulled up Eden. Marah's right shoulder hurt like it had been hit with a baseball bat, and the bright sunlight caused her to squint. Once her eyes adjusted to the light, she could see that Eden also had a bloody lip and nose. Then she looked toward the bow.

She saw a large, crescent-shaped island in the distance, covered with thick, black-green vegetation.

CHAPTER EIGHT

They anchored the boat close to shore. The man with the bloodshot eyes and the bearded man helped Marah and Eden climb off the boat and into the chest-high water, and the teenager followed, carrying the tote and Marah's duffel bag.

Marah began to feel numb. The adrenalin high she'd been riding had finally begun to dissipate, and her body hurt all over from being tossed around, each individual pain bleeding into the next until she was just one dull, throbbing ache. She envisioned herself letting go, becoming dead weight and sinking toward the ocean floor. Before she could entertain the idea, though, the man with the bloodshot eyes shoved her forward.

"Move," he said.

She trudged on, struggling not to fall, and they made

their way ashore. While crossing the beach, Marah's gaze
briefly met Eden's, and he seemed to be trying to tell her
something with his eyes, though she couldn't figure out
what it was. *Is he telling me to run for it, or to fight? Or is he
trying to tell me to stay calm?* The hideous shriek of some
jungle bird snapped her from her thoughts before she
could figure it out, and she staggered onward toward the
dense jungle.

They entered the jungle and moved inland, following
a narrow trail. After just a few steps, all traces of the beach
had disappeared, and they were quickly surrounded by
black trees and dense undergrowth. The teenager led the
way, holding his FAL 7.62 out before him. Marah and
Eden followed, barefoot, sloshing their way through a
thick, ankle-deep sludge of roots, twigs, and rocks that
jabbed into the soles of their bare feet. The other two men
brought up the rear. Marah tried to pick her way around
things that might cut her, but there was too much to avoid,
and too much that she couldn't see; after a while, she gave
up, plodding onward and grimacing through the pain.

Even though it was dark in the jungle under the
canopy of trees, it was still humid and swelteringly hot. It
reminded Marah of a sauna, and she felt like she was
breathing through thick cheesecloth. Without the scarves
or headwear of their captors, they were attacked by clouds
of invisible mosquitoes and sandflies. Marah sliced open

the bottom of her foot as they crossed over some rocks, but when she paused to look at it, the man with the shaved head shoved her onward.

They continued on, over a thin, chocolate-colored stream and then up and down a series of low hills. Then they left the trail and fought through a dense stretch of undergrowth before approaching a small clearing. Marah entered the clearing first; she spotted two dilapidated thatched huts near the tree line that seemed to be sinking back into the jungle. Then she noticed a crude stone fireplace in the center of the clearing, filled with burnt cans and charred bones.

Marah looked to Eden, but before she could say anything, the man with the bloodshot eyes shoved them toward a pair of thin kamagong trees at the edge of the clearing. He then turned and gave an order in Tausug to the teenager, and the teenager disappeared into one of the thatched huts. A moment later, the teenager reemerged from the hut, holding two pairs of rusty handcuffs.

"Eden—"

Before Eden could reply, the man with the bloodshot eyes shoved Marah toward the ground.

"Down," he said.

She knelt, struggling not to fall over. Eden knelt as well. The teenager cut their zip ties, then made a hugging gesture with his arms, wrapping them around the tree.

Eden hesitated, and the man with the bloodshot eyes shoved him again, nearly knocking him over.

"Do it," he said.

Eden and Marah wrapped their arms around the trees, and the teenager handcuffed them, kneeling and facing the trees, arms wrapped around the trunks. Then the teenager joined the others by the fireplace, where they had a discussion in Tausug. Eden struggled to turn toward Marah.

"You okay?" he said.

She nodded, choking up.

"I'm so sorry," he said. "This is all my fault—"

"No, it's not—"

"Yeah, it is."

"Eden—"

"I'm gonna get us out of this, I promise—"

Before Eden could finish, the man with the bloodshot eyes fired a burst from his machine gun into the trees above them, showering them with shredded leaves and bits of exploded mabolo fruit.

"No talking," he said.

Eden spat away the splatter as the man with the bloodshot eyes resumed his conversation. Marah looked toward Eden, her eyes wide and full of fear. He nodded slowly, as if to reassure her, but once again, she didn't feel reassured. She forced a smile before turning away and looking toward the jungle.

It seemed like a thousand eyes were staring back at her.

CHAPTER NINE

At night, the jungle came alive again with a myriad of sounds. Primates chattered high up in the trees; birds cried out in the darkness, sometimes answered by others, and sometimes not. A flying fox screeched past overhead and went crashing through the foliage, grabbing for low-hanging fruit with its clawed thumbs. Beneath it all, a constant chittering of centipedes, roaches, and other insects scratched away like the string section of an orchestra.

Marah leaned against the tree, struggling to find a position in which her legs wouldn't go numb. She was exhausted and wanted to sleep, but she was far too anxious and uncomfortable. Eden slept kneeling against the tree next to her, like some weary penitent, his head resting against the tree at an awkward angle. He'd tried to stay awake, but he'd somehow fallen asleep in the middle of the night, after the teenager had relieved the bearded man who'd sat the first watch at the fire.

Marah's mind was a tempest; questions ricocheted back and forth in her thoughts, bringing more questions that then brought even more questions, multiplying like splitting cells. *Who were their captors? What did they want? Where were they, and did anyone even know they were missing?* The more she dwelled on their situation, the more panicky she became. She tried to think of something else, but everything she smelled, saw, and heard brought her right back to where she was, and it was impossible to escape it.

Blood-colored hints of morning eventually began to appear in the sky, behind the initial graying flush of dawn. Fingers of soft light soon reached down through the thick canopy of trees, illuminating the darkest recesses of the jungle. The warmth of the sun slowly urged out the delicate scents of the wild coronitas, the moon orchids, and the sampaguita flowers, chasing the nighttime odors of wet, dead leaves, standing water, and the giant Rafflesia flowers that smelled like rotting corpses. Birds began to flit about, emerging from their nests and dens, and the pleasant chatter of the quetzals and kingfishers replaced the monotonous drone of the insects.

Marah watched the sunrise through the thick lattice

of branches; it was the first she'd seen in almost two decades. The last one she could recall had been on a drive to Key West with her college roommates during spring break of her junior year. She remembered how beautiful it had been at the time, rising directly ahead of them as they headed southeast along a bend in the I-95. She'd made a point to get up for sunrises more often; more than fifteen years had passed, though, and she hadn't watched a single sunrise until now.

After the sun came up, the man with the bloodshot eyes exited one of the huts and relieved himself against a rubber tree. Marah jealously watched him, her own bladder near the point of bursting. She caught a whiff of his urine, foul smelling and ammoniac even from a distance, and watched uncomfortably as it spread toward them through runnels in the mud. She breathed a sigh of relief when it changed direction before reaching her. Then she watched as the man with the bloodshot eyes went back toward the fire and took over the watch from the teenager.

The teenager fetched a dirty pot from the hut, filled it with water, and put it over the fire. Before long, the water began to boil, and the teenager used it to make instant coffee in a pair of rusty tin cups. Marah studied their captors. She struggled to follow the men's conversation, but she gleaned what she could from their body language and a few repeated words that she made out. It appeared that the one with the bloodshot eyes went by the name Wahab, while the bearded one's name was Mustafa. They called the teenager Flaco, which sounded like a nickname, and the man who'd left in their boat was called Abu Tuan or Abu Tong. She thought they might be terrorists— during the night, they'd used a battery-powered boom box to listen to a CD of what sounded like some sort of jihadist ranting—but they'd also listened to rap music and smoked thick blunts that gave off the sickly sweet smell of uncured marijuana. They might have been modern-day pirates, for all she knew; it was impossible to tell.

Soon after Wahab and Flaco finished drinking their coffee, Mustafa emerged from the other thatched hut, yawning and scratching himself. Flaco refilled the pot with water and put it back over the fire, and once it was boiling again, he made coffee for Mustafa.

Eden woke with a start and glanced around, disoriented. After he got his bearings and seemed to remember where he was, he noticed that Marah was awake.

"Did you sleep?" he said.

She shook her head.

"I'm sorry," he said.

"What for?"

"I tried to stay awake . . ."

His voice grew shaky, and he averted his eyes from her. She suddenly saw something in him that she hadn't seen in years, something soft and vulnerable. *Was it anxiety?* she wondered. *Dread?* After a moment, he looked back to her, his eyes glassy and wet.

"This is all my fault," he said.

"No, it's not," she said.

He forced a smile, and she smiled back. The moment didn't last, though; she felt the need to relieve herself again, grimacing from the pain.

"I have to go to the bathroom," she said.

Eden looked toward the men.

"Hey," he said.

They didn't reply.

"Excuse me," said Eden.

Wahab looked in their direction but didn't say anything.

"She needs to go," said Eden.

"So go," said Wahab, laughing and turning his attention back to the others.

"We can't even get our pants down," said Eden, gesturing to the handcuffs.

Wahab ignored him.

"Please," said Eden.

Wahab said something in Tausug to Mustafa, and after a moment, Mustafa got up and got his M16. He then approached Marah and unlocked her cuffs.

"You first," he said, pulling her to her feet and cuffing her hands behind her back.

Marah looked toward Eden, concerned.

"Don't worry," he said, then added in an eerily matter-of-fact way: "They need us alive."

Marah slogged her way through the ankle-deep mud, her hands cuffed behind her back. Every third or fourth step, she felt something sharp beneath one of her bare feet, but she ignored it each time and kept going. She felt light-headed and dizzy from the lack of food, water, and sleep, and it was difficult maintaining her balance with her hands cuffed. She stumbled and fell at one point, and Mustafa yanked her back to her feet and shoved her onward, grunting something in his native tongue.

They continued on. Before long, they reached a small clearing; a thin, murky stream wound its way through the clearing before disappearing beneath the undergrowth. Mustafa stopped walking.

"Go," he said.

Marah hesitated, unsure.

"Go," said Mustafa again, louder.

Marah struggled to push down her pants with her cuffed hands, but she barely even managed to move them.

"A little help?" she said.

Mustafa ignored her.

"Please," said Marah. "I won't try anything."

Mustafa continued to ignore her.

"Please," said Marah.

After a moment, Mustafa stepped forward muttering something in his native tongue and unlocked Marah's handcuffs.

"Go," he grunted again, gesturing to the stream. "Now."

Marah slowly approached the stream and squatted down, and Mustafa continued to watch, offering her no privacy. She pulled down her shorts just enough to relieve herself, keeping her eyes on Mustafa. Feeling something slippery and wet on her leg, she looked down and noticed a leech clinging to her thigh, swollen with blood.

She hesitated, suppressing the urge to vomit. After a moment, Mustafa beckoned for her to finish. She reached down and flicked at the leech, but it wouldn't come free. She flicked at it again and again, but it was firmly attached. She tried to push a fingernail underneath its sucker, but it still wouldn't let go.

Mustafa railed at Marah in his native tongue. She closed her eyes and took a deep breath, then pinched the tail of the leech and yanked it off. She flicked it into the stream and watched as it sank, writhing into the murky, brown water.

Then she looked down again and saw an inflamed area on the inside of her thigh around an oozing, y-shaped wound.

Marah sat cuffed to the kamagong tree in an awkward version of *virasana*, her knees close to each other and thighs perpendicular to the ground. She waited for Eden and Mustafa to return, occupying herself by watching the tiny spider monkeys race up and down the long branches of the kamagongs. A few minutes went by, and then a few more passed. Marah began to worry that Eden might have tried to escape, leaving her behind. *There's no way he'd do that,* she thought to herself. Then a louder yet calmer voice spoke in her thoughts: *Don't be so sure.*

She soon began to have an argument in her mind. *Why would you even think that?* she wondered. *Why not?* answered the louder voice. She felt the air beginning to escape her again and felt an anxiety attack coming on, so she tried to slow her breathing by taking deeper breaths. Her efforts to calm down just seemed to bring on the anxiety attack even quicker, and she soon found herself gasping for air.

Marah closed her eyes and practiced four-count breathing. Images of Eden running away through the jungle or lying dead on the ground and shot in the back popped into her thoughts, but she blocked them out with her slow, measured counting. Before long, she heard a branch snap in the distance, and after a moment, she opened her eyes and watched Eden emerge from the forest where he'd entered it, followed by Mustafa. Mud covered Eden's legs up to his knees, but she could tell from the look in his eyes that he was fine, or at least no worse than he'd been before he'd left. He knelt down where he'd been kneeling before, and Mustafa chained him back to the tree.

"You okay?" she asked.

He nodded.

"You?"

She nodded back. Then she watched with envy as Flaco cracked open another coconut for Mustafa, who let its juice spill down his chin and beard as he drank. Eden noticed Marah watching, and after a moment, he shouted to the men.

"Hey, what about us?"

The men ignored him.

"We haven't had anything to drink since you brought us here," he said.

The men continued to ignore him.

"Come on," he said. "We're not worth anything to you dead."

Wahab turned and said something in Tausug to

Flaco, and Flaco got up and fetched a plastic jug of what looked like river water. He brought it over to them and tossed it at the ground. Eden got as low as he could and kicked the jug toward his cuffed hands. As soon as it was in reach, he grabbed it and then extended it to Marah. She took the jug from him at looked at its murky, tea-colored contents.

"You sure we should drink this?" she asked.

"Do we have a choice?"

She didn't reply, knowing he was right. After a moment, she struggled to get the cap off the jug and raised it to her lips. It smelled like turpentine and rotten eggs.

She held her nose and drank some of it, gagging after choking it down.

The blazing midday sun broiled the jungle. It felt like being in a steam bath, and like they were drowning in hot, wet air.

Eden stared toward the horizon, lost in thought. Marah tried to sleep, but she couldn't manage, despite being exhausted. She occupied herself by watching a caterpillar crawl along a branch on one of the nearby trees. It was a fascinating-looking insect; on its eighth and ninth segments, there were white markings that looked like bird droppings, which helped it blend into the surroundings.

She watched it vanish behind a leaf, jealous of its ability to disappear.

After a while, she heard a low, whistling birdcall in the distance. Mustafa stood up and said something in Tausug to Wahab. Marah and Eden watched as Wahab cupped his hands together and made a low, whistling birdcall of his own. A moment later, Abu Tuan, carrying a dirty canvas sack, emerged from the jungle and entered the clearing. He tossed the sack to the others, and they rifled through it, wolfing down the fresh *pandesal* rolls and cans of tinned meat that he brought them.

Marah watched as the men ravaged the food, desperate for just a bite of one of the soft, pillowy rolls. She recalled the peanut-filled mochi she'd bought back in Semporna, and how she'd thrown it away without finishing it. *What a waste,* she thought to herself, a small part of her wanting to laugh while a bigger part of her wanted to cry. Before she could do either, Abu Tuan approached them and handed Eden a pad and pen.

"What's this?" asked Eden.

"Phone numbers," he said.

"What?"

"Write phone numbers," said Abu Tuan. "Whoever wants you alive."

Eden hesitated, looking to Marah.

"Go," said Abu Tuan.

Eden scribbled a name and number onto the pad and gave it back to Abu Tuan.

"Who this?" asked Abu Tuan.

"My grandmother," said Eden.

"No parents?"

Eden shook his head. "My mother's dead," he said. "I don't know where my father is."

Abu Tuan hesitated.

"I'm not lying," said Eden. "You can look it up."

Abu Tuan gave the pad and pen to Marah.

"You," he said.

She began to write, but she couldn't remember her mother's number, despite it being unchanged since she'd been in college. *Did it start with a seven?* she wondered, flabbergasted. *Or was it a nine?* Panicked, she looked to Eden.

"What is it?" he asked.

"I can't remember," she said.

"What?"

Abu Tuan spoke before she could reply.

"Hurry up," he said.

She closed her eyes and took a deep breath, trying to shut everything out as she struggled to recall the number. After a moment, the name Brendan Shanahan popped into her mind—*fourteen,* she immediately thought, remembering his uniform number and the memory technique she'd used to memorize things as a girl—and then she recalled *bicentennial*—seventy-six—along with the rest of the phone number. She quickly scribbled it down in a shaky script that looked nothing like her normal handwriting. Then she gave the pad and pen back to Abu Tuan, who read aloud what she wrote.

"Carolyn and Tom Johnston?" he said.

Marah nodded slowly, almost as if unsure of it herself. Abu Tuan studied her face for a long moment. Then he turned and said something in Tausug to the others.

CHAPTER TEN

A rail's whistling call pierced the dawn silence. After a while, another rail cried out, and soon the warblers and mynahs joined in, trying to upstage one another.

Eden rested awkwardly against his tree, fading in and out of sleep. Marah knelt against her tree, wide-awake and struggling to scratch herself despite the handcuffs. The insects had been relentless; the tiger mosquitoes had come alone, and she hadn't felt their bites until long after they'd flown away. The sand flies had come in swarms, leaving large red patches that itched even worse than the mosquito bites. The tiny ginger ants had attacked both alone and in force, their powerful stings causing a sharp, burning pain. Before dawn broke, even Marah's bites seemed to have bites, and her whole body itched and felt like it was on fire.

She'd spent another sleepless night on the treadmill of her mind. Her thoughts bounced from one negative scenario to the next, wondering how'd they'd come up with the money, what would happen if they didn't, and if they'd even leave the island alive. She'd tried to come up with something to distract herself, a snippet of a song or a prayer or even a commercial jingle, but it was no use; nothing could rise above the noise in her head.

Shortly after the first light appeared, Abu Tuan emerged from one of the huts. He shouted toward the other hut, and a moment later, Mustafa and Wahab came out and joined him and Flaco at the fire.

Marah turned to Eden. "Hey," she said.

He didn't stir, so she kicked him in the leg.

"Eden," she said.

He glanced over at her, dazed.

"Something's happening," she said.

They watched as the men spoke by the fire. After a moment, the men approached them, and Wahab pulled Marah to her feet.

"What's going on?" asked Eden.

Wahab unlocked Marah's handcuffs.

"She make phone call," he said.

"Take me—"

Mustafa kicked Eden in the side.

"Shut up," he said.

Eden slumped over, groaning. Abu Tuan tossed a bag of zip ties to Wahab, and Wahab bound Marah's wrists before shoving her toward the jungle. She glanced back at Eden, eyes wide and full of fear.

"Eden—"

He cut her off. "It's all right," he said, his words labored. "Just do what they say—"

Before Eden could finish, Abu Tuan frog-marched Marah into the jungle. After a few steps, she turned and looked back, but the clearing was already blocked from view.

Marah slogged through the jungle, back in the direction of the beach. She slipped and stumbled through the ankle-deep muck, slashing her feet on rocks, broken branches, and other detritus. Abu Tuan followed a few paces behind her. If she slowed too much or strayed from the path, he shoved her in the back or prodded her onward with the end of his gun.

Her thoughts kept returning to the clearing, and to their situation. She wondered what would happen if they didn't get the money. *Would they hurt us to send a message? And what if we don't get them what they want? Then what?*

She began to grow queasy, thinking about their bodies lying in shallow jungle graves, or at the bottom of the sea.

They soon reached the stream, and after crossing it, they picked up the narrow trail. At one point, Marah felt a leech on the back of her leg, but with her hands bound, she couldn't reach down to flick it away. *What did it even matter, anyway?* she thought to herself. Her body was already a tapestry of bites and rashes, and they had far bigger problems.

She struggled up a slight hill and down the other side. She lost her balance on the decline, and she couldn't manage to grab anything to break her fall. She fell forward and into the mud, landing hard on her shoulder and side and getting a mouthful of the gritty sludge as she sucked for air.

"Move," said Abu Tuan.

He yanked her back to her feet and they continued on. She stifled the urge to cry and then cursed herself for being so weak. She wished Eden were there with her, suddenly realizing how little she'd been thinking about him, and how much she'd been taking him for granted. *How long had it been that way?* she wondered. *Since the third miscarriage, or the second? Or even before them?* A feeling of unease came over her.

They continued their way through the jungle. Before long, Marah felt a light breeze through the kamagong trees, and soon after that, she could smell the salty tang of the ocean. They went up another short hill and then came down the other side. Through the thinning jungle, Marah spotted the beach and the endless blue sea just beyond it, shimmering like a mirage.

They emerged from the trees and made their way down toward the water. Out in the open, it felt cooler than it did in the jungle interior, and Marah's spirits began to lift. The moment was short-lived, however; she turned her ankle in the powdery sand near the top of the beach, and she fell again, landing hard on her side and losing her breath. Abu Tuan pulled her to her feet.

"Keep moving," he said.

He shoved her onward again, and they soon approached the sea. Marah spotted the boat they'd arrived in, anchored about a hundred feet from shore. When she reached the water, she turned to Abu Tuan, expecting him to cut the zip tie, but instead, he pushed her into the water.

"Go on," he said.

Marah waded out toward the boat. The water felt heavenly, a soothing balm upon her burning skin. When the water reached her chest, she felt tempted to lean down and take a drink, but as thirsty as she was, she fought off the urge, knowing salt water would only dehydrate her. She leaned her head back when the water reached her chin, then stood on her tiptoes and closed her mouth when it approached her lips. Abu Tuan held the M16 above water with one hand while guiding Marah with the other. He pulled himself up onto the boat first and then reached down for her once he was aboard. After Abu Tuan pulled Marah onto the boat, he pushed her toward the hull.

"Lie down," he said.

Marah got down on her knees, then bent forward and dropped to her side. Abu Tuan unfurled the blue tarp and covered her. After a moment, she heard him start one of the outboard motors and then the other, and another moment later, they were moving.

Marah felt the boat swing around and begin to head away from the island. She wondered if they were heading back toward Sabah, or if they were heading toward one of the islands in the Mindanao chain. She tried to get a glimpse of the direction they were heading, but all she could see between the edge of the tarp and the hull was a sliver of the cloudless sky. She struggled to turn over and looked out through a gap on the other side, but again, there was nothing to see.

She grew seasick and felt her airways constricting. Their speed increased, and the light boat was soon flying across the waves. The thin bottom of the boat smacked down against a trough, and then another, and Marah saw stars when her head slammed into the hull. She closed her eyes and took a deep breath, suddenly recalling a line from Emily Dickinson's "'Hope' is the thing with feathers," a poem she'd studied as an undergraduate. She began to whisper the lines of the poem in order to calm herself.

> *"Hope" is the thing with feathers —*
> *That perches in the soul —*
> *And sings the tune without the words —*
> *And never stops — at all —*

It seemed to be helping, so she recited the poem again, and then a third time.

After she got her breathing back under control, Marah started to count out the seconds in her head; if she couldn't see where they were heading, she could at least approximate how long it would take them to get there. The engines were so loud that she felt like she was shouting just to keep count, but she stayed as focused as she could. She soon reached a count of a thousand, and then passed two thousand, and then three.

Shortly after she reached a count of nine thousand, and after she'd hit her head against the hull three more times, the roar of the engines diminished to a whimper, and the boat began to slow. Marah stopped counting and did the math in her head. If her seconds were anywhere close to actual seconds, they'd been traveling for almost three hours.

She soon felt the boat gently bump up against something—a dock, maybe—and then felt the boat dip slightly as if Abu Tuan had disembarked. She felt the boat being tied to something, and a moment later, the boat dipped again when it felt like Abu Tuan had stepped back aboard.

Abu Tuan pulled the tarp off her, and she looked up at him, squinting from the bright sunlight.

"Get up," he said.

Marah sat up, and Abu Tuan pulled her to her feet. She glanced around at their surroundings; the boat was moored to a small wooden dock at a rocky, trash-strewn beach. Inland, all she could see was a tangle of palm trees and more dense jungle. It was impossible for her to tell whether it was Malaysia or the Philippines.

Abu Tuan placed the M16 at the bottom of the hull where Marah had been and covered it with the tarp. For a moment, she thought Abu Tuan might be going inland unarmed, but he reached into a plastic milk crate and pulled out a scuffed pistol, which he stuffed into his waistband. Then he shoved Marah toward the dock.

"Go," he said.

Marah stepped onto the dock, relieved to be back on solid ground. Then she felt guilty, remembering that Eden was back in the jungle somewhere, alone. Abu Tuan stepped onto the dock and dropped a pair of worn rubber sandals at her feet, then nodded toward them. She struggled into the sandals; they were a size too small for her, but she was grateful to have footwear.

"Move," said Abu Tuan, shoving her forward again.

They walked to the end of the dock and stepped onto land. Abu Tuan pushed Marah toward the entrance to a narrow path at the top of the beach, and she followed the path through the sparse jungle. They continued along the trail until it reached a cul-de-sac at the end of a narrow dirt road.

Marah spotted a rusty white Honda Prelude with no hubcaps and a black trunk lid parked on the shoulder of the road. She noticed it had the same simple black-and-white license plates she remembered seeing back in Tawau and Semporna; she wasn't sure if that meant they were in Malaysia or not, though, since she didn't know what the license plates looked like in the Philippines.

Abu Tuan approached the Prelude and opened its trunk, then turned to Marah.

"In," he said.

She hesitated, her knees buckling.

"Please—"

Abu Tuan shoved her into the trunk before she could finish. Panicking, Marah instinctively tried to get back out of it, but he shoved her down again, pushing her head against the floor. Unlike the hull of the boat, the trunk was a much tighter space, hardly bigger than she was, and something blunt pushed into her lower back. It smelled like something had died in there, and she looked up at Abu Tuan with pleading eyes.

"Wait—" she began.

Before she could finish, he shut the trunk lid, and everything went black.

CHAPTER ELEVEN

Marah rode in the trunk, lying on her side. It felt like an oven, heated by the sun. She could see a bit after her eyes adjusted to the near-darkness; some light leaked in around the keyhole and through a few cracks. She spotted some empty plastic bottles, a burlap sack, and a rusty bicycle lock. Then she noticed a stuffed sheep wedged in the wheel well of the trunk and she shuddered, wondering what had happened to its owner.

The car's shocks were badly worn, and Marah bounced up and down along the dirt road, hitting her shoulder and head against the trunk lid and floor. She reached around with her bound hands, searching for something sharp to cut the zip tie with, but there was nothing of any use. *And even if I'd found something,* she wondered, *would I try to cut myself free, knowing I'd have nowhere to go and nothing to fight him with?*

She felt herself growing sick again and her breath getting short, so she resumed reciting the Dickinson poem in an attempt to calm herself. Once she got her breathing under control, she began counting again. After a while, the ride went from bumpy to smooth; Marah assumed they'd gone from a dirt road to a paved one. Not long after she'd counted to six hundred, they stopped and made a right-hand turn. After she'd reached a thousand, they made another right-hand turn, and just before she'd gotten to thirteen hundred, they turned left, and the car came to a stop.

Marah heard the car engine shut off. She listened for sounds or clues to their location, but she couldn't hear anything other than the faint, far-off drone of a passing airplane. After what felt like an eternity, she heard a car door open, and then she heard footsteps approaching on what sounded like loose gravel. It reminded her of the scratching, dragging sounds from the horror movies she'd watched with her sister as a girl, and it made her skin crawl.

A moment later, the trunk lid opened and sunlight flooded in, forcing Marah to squint again. She looked up and saw Abu Tuan standing over her, holding a plastic shopping bag. A run-down concrete building stood nearby, rusty rebar jutting up like wilted corn stalks from its top floor. It looked like they were in an alley.

"Out," he said.

Marah struggled to raise herself, realizing that her right leg had fallen asleep during the ride. Abu Tuan pulled her out of the trunk and to her feet, where she leaned against the car for support. Then he fanned open a balisong and spun her around, slitting the zip tie with a flick of the balisong's blade before turning her back around to face him. He then reached into his plastic bag and pulled out a black abaya and hijab and a pair of cheap aviator sunglasses, which he shoved into her hands.

"Put them on," he said.

She took them from him and began to dress. She struggled with the hijab, unsure how to wrap it. Abu Tuan took it from her and properly fashioned it, gently folding the scarf from the top right corner to the bottom left corner, placing it over her head, and then wrapping it loosely under her chin before pinning back the ends. His tender gesture startled her, and she felt herself growing unsteady and weak.

Abu Tuan spoke. "Phone here. We call you family. No talk, no look, no run, or you husband dead. Understand?"

Marah nodded. Abu Tuan grunted and shoved her

toward the end of the alley.

"Go," he said.

They left the alley and emerged onto a pocked and roughly paved road. Marah studied their surroundings as they made their way through the small town; unlike Semporna, there were no new buildings, dive centers, or western tourists — it looked like something from a simpler past or some post-apocalyptic near future. The majority of the people were Bajau and Buginese peasants, mostly women, some dressed in abaya and hijab while others wore colorful T-shirts and shorts. The remainder were Malay and Chinese and appeared wealthier and more modern than the Bajau and Buginese, judging by their fancier clothes and cell phones.

They followed the street toward a block that seemed to be the center of town. A run-down, two-story building stood on one side of the street, while a row of small shops lined the opposite side. Marah followed Abu Tuan across the street, and they passed a wet market full of locals selling fresh fish and cassava crackers in stalls made of framing planks and corroded zinc sheets. She tried to make eye contact with one of the women, pleading to her with her eyes, but the woman looked away.

Passing a storefront window, Marah caught a glimpse of her own reflection, realizing that in the hijab, abaya, and sunglasses, she was practically invisible.

The phone booth stood at a corner of an empty lot, near a crumbling, cinder block wall. Graffiti-scrawled, battered by the elements, and dappled with bird droppings, it looked like it had survived an atomic blast and was the only thing in the area that had remained standing.

Abu Tuan stopped Marah before she could reach the phone booth.

"Wait," he said.

She waited as he approached the phone booth and picked up the receiver, and she glanced around at their surroundings, looking for street signs, license plates, or anything that might reveal their location. She saw an abandoned shack across the way, a feral dog poking among some trash, and some crumpled Tiger beer cans in the dry weeds, but other than that, nothing gave clues to their location. It was just some anonymous, backwater village, one of thousands dotting the Malaysian and Filipino coastlines.

After a moment, Abu Tuan began talking over the phone. Marah strained to listen, overhearing the phrases "two million" and "three days." She scanned the area again, spotting a passing pickup truck. Its rust-eaten license plate was dented and hard to make out, but it looked similar to the ones she'd seen back in Semporna. She tried to make eye contact with the driver, but he stared ahead as he drove past.

A moment later, Abu Tuan rested the receiver atop the cradle hook and approached Marah. He pulled her toward the phone and shoved the receiver into her hand.

"Tell them you okay," he said, holding her tightly by the upper arm.

Marah raised the phone to her ear. "Hello?" she said, hoping to hear her mother's voice. Instead, her stepfather answered.

"Marah?" he said. "Are you all right?"

His voice flustered her. *Of course he'd take the phone,* she thought to herself, growing enraged. *He always has to be in control.* She heard her mother asking for the phone in the background, then felt herself shrinking as she'd done since she was a teenager, whenever they'd argued. She could see them standing in the dining room of their sterile McMansion, her mother in a drab nightgown that made her look twenty years older than she actually was, reaching for the phone, and her stepfather holding out an extended, upturned hand to her like some officious traffic cop. She grit her teeth, angry with her stepfather for being so controlling, and angry with her mother for being so submissive.

"I'm fine," said Marah. "We're okay."

Abu Tuan spoke. "Tell him no contact authorities."

Tom replied before Marah could. "Where are you?"

Abu Tuan tightened his grip on Marah's arm. "Go

on," he said. "Tell him."

"Don't contact the authorities," she said.

"If he do, we kill you," said Abu Tuan.

Before she could say it, she heard her mother's frail voice in the background.

"Honey—?"

An unexpected sob rose in Marah's throat.

"Tell him!" said Abu Tuan.

Marah spoke again into the receiver, struggling to spit out the words. "They'll kill us if you do—"

Abu Tuan grabbed the phone before Marah could finish. "Get the money," he said.

Then he hung up without waiting for a reply.

They made their way back across the small town. Questions flooded Marah's mind. *Will my mother panic and go to the police? Have they already gone to the authorities? Do they have anywhere close to the amount he asked for, and even if they do, will we make it out of this alive?* She began to feel dizzy and weak again. Focusing on her surroundings instead, she resumed looking for clues to their location. She soon spotted a building that read *"PORTAL RASMI HOSPITAL KUNAK"* in maroon lettering, then saw a middle school farther up the street with a sign outside that read *"SMK KUNAK JAYA."* She remembered seeing a sign for Kunak as they were leaving Semporna. *Was it farther up the coast from Semporna, or was it south, in the direction of the*

Indonesian border? She couldn't remember.

They eventually reached the alley where the Prelude was parked. After approaching the car, Abu Tuan unlocked the trunk and turned to Marah.

"Get in," he said.

She hesitated again, and he shoved her into the trunk, where she bumped her head against a spare tire. She tried to turn over, getting tangled up in the hijab in the process, but he pushed her down onto her stomach. Then he slipped a zip tie over her wrists, pulled it tight, and shut the trunk lid over her.

Marah spat the hijab out of her mouth and listened as the driver-side door opened and closed. A moment later, the car shuddered to life, and they began moving again. She laid there, eyes closed, gritting her teeth so she wouldn't scream. She bit down so hard that she could taste her own enamel, bitter and gritty. After a moment, she unclenched her jaws, but as soon as she did, she felt the urge to hyperventilate, so she bit down again and kept her mouth shut. After a few minutes, they made a right-hand turn, and the car came to a stop. Marah could hear Abu Tuan get out of the car and approach the trunk again.

"Any noise, you dead," he said.

He started to walk away, and when she could no longer hear his footsteps, she rolled over and looked toward the keyhole. She couldn't see anything other than a section of a palm tree—it looked so strange and so innocuous, like an image in the background of a travel agency advertisement. She fantasized about escaping, envisioning herself forcing open the trunk.

A moment later, she heard footsteps approaching the car again. Then she heard Abu Tuan get in and restart the car's engine.

CHAPTER TWELVE

They rode for a while along a straightaway, turned twice in quick succession, and then traveled some more along a rougher route. After the car bottomed out against what felt like a pothole, the stuffed sheep bounced over Marah's back and into her sightline. Its black plastic eyes seemed to stare back at her, and even though she knew that wasn't possible, it continued to unnerve her until she felt another panic attack developing.

She tried to nudge the stuffed sheep away, but she couldn't reach it, so she rolled over and turned her back to it, focusing instead on the trunk lid. She studied its scratches and dents to take her mind off things. One long, curving gash reminded her of the Delaware River from a map she'd had on her bedroom wall as a girl; another scratch looked like a lightning bolt, and a dent looked like a side of beef. No matter what she did, though, her thoughts kept returning to the stuffed sheep, which reminded her of a toy lamb she'd purchased during her first pregnancy. Like many first-time mothers-to-be, she'd gone overboard with her preparations; she'd bought clothes in every size from zero to three months up to two years, choosing gender-neutral colors and patterns, as it had been too early to determine the sex. She'd purchased baby monitors and a Swedish high chair, an expensive new crib and strollers for every occasion and terrain. She'd even chosen names; if it had been a girl, she'd wanted the name Madeline Olivia, after her two grandmothers, and if it had been a boy, she'd wanted to name him Carter. She'd told Eden she'd found the name on a family tree, which wasn't a lie — there was an Edward Carter Lafarge on her mother's side, back in the mid-1800s. She couldn't care less about Edward Carter Lafarge, though, a flour merchant in St. Louis who'd had thirteen children with three different wives. She'd wanted the name because of Carter Exley, a boy she'd been involved with during the eighth grade, the year before her father died; she'd sat next to him in English class, and he'd encouraged her to try out with him for the school production of *Grease*, in which they'd been cast as the leads. He was her first real crush and the first boy she'd ever French-kissed. He'd moved away before freshman year, though, and they'd eventually lost touch; years later, while at NYU, she'd heard he'd gotten a girl pregnant and had moved to Arizona to work for her father's air-conditioning business. After she'd lost the baby sixteen weeks into the pregnancy — after discovering it had been a boy — she'd blamed herself, believing it'd been her fault for lying, at least by omission, about her true motivation for its name. When she'd gotten pregnant again the following year, she'd chosen different names — Martin, after Eden's grandfather, and Amelia, after her great aunt. She'd lost that baby, too, only fourteen weeks into the pregnancy, after which she'd gotten rid of all the baby clothes, toys, and furniture, including the plush toy lamb, believing they were somehow cursed. The third time she'd gotten pregnant, she hadn't even bothered coming up with names, unwilling to become attached.

Abu Tuan made one more stop on the way back to the dock. While he was gone, Marah didn't even bother fantasizing about escaping, knowing that she wouldn't try. When Abu Tuan returned after a few minutes, Marah could smell that he had some sort of hot, greasy food — hamburgers, or maybe fried chicken. It smelled incredible, and before long, she was salivating. She tried to focus on the trunk lid again, but all she could see in its scratches and dents were French fries and chicken wings. Her stomach muscles contracted, and she felt shaky and weak, so she resumed counting.

She knew they were getting close when they went from a paved road to a dirt one, and she soon found herself getting tossed and jostled around with each pothole and divot in the terrain. Before long, the car came to a stop, and after Abu Tuan shut off the engine and opened the driver-side door, Marah envisioned Eden throwing open the trunk and yelling "*Surprise!*" back in Shanghai, surrounded by their friends. But Eden didn't open the trunk, Abu Tuan did, and they weren't back in Shanghai; they were at the end of the dirt road.

"Out," said Abu Tuan.

Marah struggled out of the trunk and to her feet, and Abu Tuan nodded toward the narrow path leading back to the beach. They made their way through the sparse jungle; Abu Tuan carried a plastic bag filled with cigarettes, energy drinks, and more of the fluffy *pandesal* rolls he'd brought before. The smell of them reminded Marah of the New York City bakeries at dawn, and it made her stomach roil again. Trying to take her mind off it, she looked down at her feet and focused on her footsteps.

They soon reached the docks and got onto the boat. Abu Tuan pushed Marah toward the hull.

"Lie down," he said.

She got down on her knees, bent forward, and dropped to her side. Abu Tuan unfurled the blue tarp over her, and after a moment, she could hear him start the outboard motors.

Another moment later, they were moving, and the boat turned around in a slow, lilting arc. Once Abu Tuan had it pointing away from the beach, he hit the engines, and they were soon flying across the waves. Before long, Marah began hyperventilating; the movement, the smells of the food and the sea, and the physical duress and lack of sleep were all too much for her. She closed her eyes and tried to slow her breathing by doing some four-count exercises, but it didn't help, so she resumed reciting the Dickinson poem. She went through the poem four times until her breathing finally slowed. Then she started counting again. After she passed a thousand, they caught air at the top of a high wave and came down hard against a trough, and Marah got thrown from one side of the hull to the other. She smashed her head against the hull and saw stars once more.

She continued counting the seconds in her head. Her counting reached two thousand again, and then four thousand, and then six. The boat finally began to slow after she'd reached a count of eighty-six hundred; she assumed she might've been counting a bit faster than before, or perhaps they weren't fighting currents or headwinds going back. Either way, she figured the trip once again took them around three hours. It was hard to guess how fast they were traveling, but if they were doing about thirty knots, that put them somewhere around a hundred miles from Sabah.

Marah heard a splash and felt the boat stop drifting. Abu Tuan pulled the tarp off her and hauled her to her feet.

"Up," he said.

They dropped into the water and slowly made their way to shore. Marah lost one of her rubber sandals tripping over some coral, but when she stopped to get it, Abu Tuan shoved her onward.

"Go," he said.

They trudged up the beach and entered the jungle. Somewhere behind them, the sun sank toward the ocean, hidden by the trees, and its light began to fade from the jungle. Marah struggled to make her way through the sludge with only one ill-fitting sandal, slipping and sliding through the muck. She eventually just kicked it off and left it behind, finding it easier to continue on barefoot.

Before long, Marah spotted a hill she remembered descending on their way out of the camp. Then she saw the gnarled roots of a massive tipolo tree she recalled passing that had a large skull-shaped patch on its bark. A few dozen paces later, Abu Tuan cupped his hands over his mouth and made a low, whistling birdcall. After a moment, they heard a low, whistling call in reply.

They fought their way through the last stretch of undergrowth and soon reached the clearing. Wahab stood by the fire, rolling a cigarette. Marah scanned the area for Eden, her airways constricting when she didn't seem him by the rubber trees. She glanced around, breathing easier when she saw him chained to another tree.

Abu Tuan shoved Marah toward Eden. He looked up at her—his arms, legs, and face were reddened with sunburn, and his lips looked like a dry riverbed, swollen and cracked. Abu Tuan cut Marah's zip tie, pushed her down, and chained her to a tree before joining Wahab by the fire. Flaco emerged from a hut and joined them as well, leaving Marah and Eden alone.

After a moment, Eden spoke, his voice a dry rasp.

"You okay?" he said.

Marah nodded, struggling to hold it together, but she couldn't help but burst into sobs.

"Baby—"

"I'm scared," she said.

"We're gonna get out of this—"

"How?"

"I don't know, but we will."

"You keep saying that—"

Before he could reply, Mustafa emerged from the jungle, carrying a writhing monitor lizard by its long tail. He approached the others by the fire and set it down upon a large rock, where it struggled in his grasp. Even from the other side of the clearing, Marah could hear the scratching of its nails as it clawed for purchase, struggling to get away.

Mustafa took out his machete and slowly raised it. Then he took aim and chopped off the lizard's head with one swift stroke.

CHAPTER THIRTEEN

The waning moon hid behind the trees and clouds, a faint gray rumor in a sea of darkness. Somewhere out in the jungle, a frog bellowed every few seconds, hoping to attract a female.

Marah sat chained to the tree, staring at the fire, where Flaco and Mustafa shared a joint. Eden sat chained to a tree near her, sleeping fitfully in an awkward position. Two sleepless days had passed since she'd made the call to her mother and stepfather, and her mind buzzed with thoughts. She worried about her mother, who was generally set off by even the smallest of troubles, like flight delays or late mail. She worried about her health, too — she'd had diarrhea for days, a rash was spreading across her stomach and arms, and she'd surely picked up something through all the cuts in her legs and feet; she'd felt nauseous since the ordeal began, even though she couldn't remember the last time she'd eaten. Then it occurred to her that she hadn't thought much about Eden since they'd been kidnapped, and she started to worry about that, too. She remembered something her friend Lisa had said back in Shanghai, after going through a divorce; one of the things Lisa had discovered during counseling was that somewhere along the way, she and her husband had stopped thinking about their life together and were only thinking about their own selves, and their own needs.

She told herself that she was just panicking again and pushed the thought from her mind, focusing on the situation. *Maybe my mother and stepfather have come up with the money*, she figured. *But what if my stepfather doesn't have it, or what if he tries to play hardball? What if our captors don't get what they want, what then? Will there be more negotiations, or will the men be forced to act?*

At some point during the night, she finally dozed off for the first time in days, lulled into a light and fitful sleep by the steady grinding of the insects. She soon dreamed that she was diving again, wandering with Eden through the labyrinth of limestone caverns. They pushed farther and deeper into the underwater maze, eventually reaching a point where two tunnels diverged. Marah entered one tunnel while Eden entered the other, and she followed it as far as she could until she reached a large chamber full of scattered turtle bones. She noticed a pile of rocks at the other end of the chamber. She changed directions and swam toward them, expecting to find more cannonballs or ballast stones like the ones they'd found at the Portuguese wreck. After she reached them, she brushed away a thin veil of sand that covered them. Instead of finding a cannonball, though, she saw a curled-up, stillborn fetus.

Beneath it laid another stillborn fetus, and another, and another.

Marah woke with a start to the sound of her handcuffs being unlocked. Squinting through the sunlight, she saw Wahab standing over her.

"Let's go," he said, yanking her to her feet.

She turned to Eden, who was already awake.

"Where are you taking her?" he asked.

Without replying, Wahab pushed Marah toward one of the huts. Eden struggled against his handcuffs.

"Marah!" he shouted.

Before Marah could reply, Wahab forced her into a hut, where Abu Tuan was setting up a camera tripod. He spoke without looking up at them.

"Leave us," he said.

Wahab exited the hut, closing the thatched door

behind him. Marah glanced around at the surroundings. It wasn't like she'd expected; for some reason, she'd envisioned a cramped, dirty space, furnished by nothing but a prayer mat and some weapons, perhaps a jihadist banner draped over one wall. Instead, there was an inflatable mattress complete with fitted sheets, a tablet computer, some porn and soccer magazines, and some cases of energy drinks. Abu Tuan looked up at her, registering her surprise.

"Like movies?" he asked.

She didn't reply.

"It's okay," said Abu Tuan, going back to setting up the tripod. "I hate movies. Especially American movies, where everyone got perfect teeth and good guys always win."

Again, Marah said nothing, stifling the urge to be sick. After a moment, Abu Tuan continued. "When I was boy, my mother take me to American movies," he said. "Every Sunday. Like church to her. She dress up, hope some GI notice. Sometime, they do, but they never serious. After they fuck her in alley, or in car, they disappear. She just a trophy to them."

Marah still didn't reply, growing more and more uncomfortable the longer Abu Tuan talked.

"There was one movie I like," he said, "but I don't see with my mother. My friend bring it back from Manila.

Faces of Death. You know this movie?"

She said nothing, though she'd heard some boys discussing it when she'd been in junior high, and she remembered feeling nauseous about it even then.

"It show people die," said Abu Tuan. "Real die. Car crash, shoot-out, execution. No one look good or give speech or save day. They just die, in ugly, messy way. I can still see them in my dream."

Abu Tuan finished setting up the tripod. Then he stood up.

"That's why this easy," he said. "You no act, no look good, no think of things to say. Just tell truth, and truth is you family don't get me two million, we send you back to them piece by piece over next twenty years. Understand?"

Marah nodded, sick to her stomach.

"Good," he said. Then he gestured toward a mark on the dirt floor. "Now stand there."

Eden sat cuffed to the tree, watching the huts. After a long moment, Wahab exited one of them. Marah unsteadily followed, eyes puffy and red from crying and her face chalk-pale.

Wahab led her toward the edge of the clearing and cuffed her back to the tree.

"You okay?" asked Eden.

Marah nodded, averting her eyes from him.

"You sure?" said Eden.

She nodded again, turning her back. Then she looked down at her trembling hands.

CHAPTER FOURTEEN

They roasted underneath the midday sun. Even though
only a few fractured rays of light reached them, its heat
covered them like a pile of blankets. It reminded Marah of
the Bikram yoga she'd done in her twenties; she'd take
classes with a friend, cycling through ninety minutes of
cobra and locust poses in the sweltering, 104-degree heat.
It all seemed so absurd to her now, cuffed to a tree in some
Southeast Asian jungle.

She studied the men while Flaco cooked for them. She
noticed how interested Flaco was in the gangsta rap—he
seemed to know all the lyrics by heart and would beatbox
along to the thumping baselines—and she also noticed
how uninterested he was in the fanatical ranting of the
jihadists. She spotted additional differences as well—and

not just superficial ones, like his lighter-skinned, Zamboangueño appearance and his Hispanic accent, but emotional ones, too. He seemed vulnerable, somehow, and less hardened than the others; he didn't share the brutal shorthand they had, and he seemed like he'd come from another world.

After the men ate their lunch, Flaco brought Marah and Eden small bowls of watery rice, their first meal in days. They greedily scooped it up with their fingers, afraid it might be taken away at any moment. Halfway through, Marah saw what looked like rat droppings in the thin gruel. For a moment, she thought about saying something, but then thought better of it and picked it out.

Then she lapped up the gluey water that remained at the bottom of the bowl.

Shadows rose and flattened out before disappearing into the burgeoning night. Far-off, flapping wings sounded like faint bursts of applause, and the cooling jungle smelled like asphalt at the beginning of a rain shower.

Marah knelt against the tree, struggling to swat at mosquitoes and biting flies while continuing to watch the men. Eden knelt against his own tree, shifting from one side to the other in an attempt to find the least painful position. In the center of the clearing, Flaco and Wahab played soccer for a while, using an improvised ball made of old plastic bags and twine. After the ball started to come apart, they abandoned their game and joined Mustafa at the fire, where they listened to some fundamentalist ranting on the boom box. The men grew restless before it finished playing, and Wahab put in a Pinoy gangsta rap CD instead.

Mustafa took out a small pouch and rolled a thick blunt as a heavy baseline thumped out over the speakers. He and Wahab smoked it down to a nub before giving the roach to Flaco. After Flaco finished the joint, Mustafa ordered him to fetch some coconuts, and Flaco shinnied up a nearby tree, hacking down a half-dozen with his rusty bolo knife. Then he gathered them and brought them over to the fire, where he cracked them open and distributed them to the others.

Marah watched jealously as the men guzzled the fresh juice. Beyond parched, her swollen tongue felt like a sand-filled sock, and just thinking about the coconuts made her want to choke. She felt rage at the men, but unable to do anything with it, the feeling quickly turned to sadness, and she began to tear up. Eden noticed, and he shouted to the men.

"Hey," he said, his voice little more than a hoarse croak.

The men paid him no mind.

"Come on," said Eden. "We're dying here."

Mustafa stood and slowly walked over to them, his eyes bloodshot from the marijuana. He grinned and said something in his native tongue, something Marah assumed to be mocking.

"Have a heart," said Eden.

Mustafa gestured to his coconut, and Eden nodded. Mustafa then raised the coconut and guzzled its remains, the juices spilling down his chin and chest. Then he turned over the coconut, letting the last few drops of juice fall to the mud.

"Motherfucker," said Eden.

Mustafa laughed, grinning. Then he dropped the husk to the mud before turning and heading back to the fire. Eden crouched down as low as he could and reached for the husk with one of his feet. He kicked it until it was close enough that he could reach it with his hands, then picked it up and offered it to Marah.

"Go on," he said. "There's still meat in it."

Before she could reply, he tossed it to her, and after fumbling it and then picking it up, she dug out some of the unripe coconut. Gelatinous and more sour than sweet, it still tasted delicious, and she had to stop herself from eating it all.

After a few more bites, she offered the coconut back to Eden, but he shook his head.

"You finish it," he said.

"Eden—"

"Go on," he said, smiling.

"You sure?"

He nodded. She smiled back, grateful. Then she dug out the rest of the coconut meat, and after finishing it, she licked her fingers, not wanting to waste a single shred or drop. After Mustafa finished another coconut, he tossed the empty husk into the fire and retired into one of the thatched huts. Flaco followed, retreating into the other hut. The fire died down, and the darkness began to close in around them.

Eden bent down in a modified child's pose and closed his eyes, and before long, he was soundly asleep. Marah listened to her husband's steady breathing and watched his thin back rise and fall. She studied his face, which had softened a bit and made him appear boy-like. It'd been a long time since she'd seen him fight for her, and she'd forgotten how tender he could be; in the early days of their relationship, he'd make scrambled eggs for her in the morning, and he'd often brought her flowers that he'd stolen from one of the neighborhood gardens. He'd even carried her piggyback for six city blocks once, in the rain, when she'd sprained an ankle in Central Park. These things had gotten lost somehow among their numerous moves, her miscarriages, and their financial struggles, but watching him sleep, they all came back to her, and she remembered why she'd fallen in love with him in the first place. *Would they be able to get back to that place again?* she wondered. *Why not?* some part of her answered in her thoughts, before another part added, *Assuming that you get out of this jungle alive, that is.*

Marah turned and looked toward the night sky. It could have been ten o'clock, midnight, or even two in the morning; without a watch or a clear sight of the moon, it was impossible to tell. She looked back toward the fire, where Wahab sat with the FAL 7.62 in his hands, studying them with his wide, bloodshot eyes.

Then she turned away and closed her eyes, trying to sleep.

She woke to the sound of soft tapping. At first, it sounded like someone was working on a typewriter nearby, but she noticed that the sounds were coming from all directions, and that they were more liquid than mechanical. She soon felt a drop of water hit her cheek, and then another hit her neck, and opening her eyes, she noticed a light rain falling. The sun wasn't yet up, but rumors of its arrival were everywhere, in the cobalt coloring of the sky and in the rising chorus of the morning birds.

She looked toward the fire, where Flaco sat watch, his

machine gun across his lap. After a while, she heard Abu Tuan's birdcall in the distance. Flaco stood and responded with the same call, and Mustafa and Wahab soon emerged from the huts.

Eden woke to see Abu Tuan entering the camp. Abu Tuan approached the others, immediately launching into a heated discussion in Tausug.

"What's happening?" asked Marah.

"I don't know," said Eden, "but it doesn't seem good."

Before Marah could reply, Mustafa grabbed his machine gun and stormed toward them, shouting and pointing his machine gun at Marah's head.

"Wait," she said, cowering and closing her eyes.

Mustafa pressed the end of the machine against her skull, continuing to rail at her in Tausug.

"Don't shoot!" said Eden, struggling against his restraints.

Wahab and Flaco pulled Mustafa away. He fought until Wahab said something in Tausug, then lowered his gun and backed off, cursing, as Abu Tuan turned to face Marah.

"Your parents no love you?" he asked.

"I beg your pardon?"

"Five hundred thousand is most they do, and they have million-dollar house?"

Eden spoke. "How—?"

Abu Tuan interrupted him. "You think we amateur?" he said. "We know how much Tom Johnston make, how much he have in bank. We know he have house in Vail."

"There must be some misunderstanding—"

"Yes, is misunderstanding," said Abu Tuan, interrupting her. "They no get who in charge."

"I can talk to them," she said.

"You already talk."

"Let me try," said Eden.

"You?"

"I'm a trader. It's my job to make deals."

Mustafa started to say something in Tausug, but Eden interrupted him.

"Please," he said. "I can convince them."

Abu Tuan hesitated, mulling it over.

"Come on," said Eden. "What have you got to lose?"

Abu Tuan hesitated another moment, then turned and gave an order in Tausug to the others. Marah looked toward Eden as Wahab disappeared into a hut.

"You sure about this?" she said.

Eden nodded. "What other choice do we have?"

Wahab returned with zip ties, then unlocked Eden's handcuffs and bound his wrists before him.

"Let's go," said Abu Tuan, yanking Eden to his feet.

"Eden—"

"Just do what they say," he said, interrupting her.

Before she could reply, Abu Tuan shoved Eden into the jungle. Marah turned and looked toward the other men, meeting Mustafa's gaze.

He smiled back at her, revealing his crooked, jack-o'-lantern grin.

CHAPTER FIFTEEN

The heat rose with the sun, evaporating the rain and
chasing the animals back to their warrens and dens. Thin
clouds passed by overhead, barely visible through the
thick roofing of trees, but they drifted away as quickly as
they'd arrived, doing little to hinder the sun.

Marah leaned against the tree, broiling in the heat.
She tried to clear her throat, but she was so parched that
she couldn't swallow. She glanced around at her options:
the jug of water was empty, and there were some moist
palm fronds at the edge of the forest, but they were well
out of reach. She looked toward the center of the clearing,
where Flaco gathered wood while Mustafa rested against
the side of a hut, drinking from a coconut and sunning
himself. Wahab had gone off into the jungle during the

morning and had yet to return.

Marah called to the men.

"Can I have something to drink?"

Mustafa laughed.

"Please," she said.

"Please," he replied, mimicking her. "Please!"

Ignoring him, she turned away. Mustafa shouted at Flaco, and after a moment, Flaco grabbed his gun and headed off into the jungle. Marah looked around for other options. Before long, she spotted some of the kamagong fruit in the undergrowth nearby. She stretched her foot toward them, but they were too far away to grasp, so she lowered herself as close to the ground as possible. Then she stretched for the fruit again, managing to pull one toward her with her foot.

As soon as it was close enough, Marah grabbed the fruit, only to realize that it was rotten. She tossed it aside and went through the process again, and when she got a piece of fruit that wasn't rotten, she peeled it and wolfed it down, fighting the urge to gag. After she finished eating, Marah looked over and saw Mustafa watching her, his right hand down his pants, pumping furiously at his crotch. She looked away in disbelief, but she couldn't help but look back at him, horrified to see that he was indeed masturbating in front of her, and that she hadn't imagined it. She turned away again and closed her eyes, disgusted and in shock, but she could still hear him.

"Stop it," she said, but he ignored her, continuing to grunt and pump away. She said it again, louder, but she still heard him, groaning, his tempo increasing. Finally, she just screamed out as loud as she could.

"Stop it!"

Again, Mustafa continued to ignore her until he came, moaning. Marah started to sob, but when she heard him laughing at her, her sadness turned to rage. She turned to him and shouted through the tears.

"You motherfucker!"

He laughed even harder, which further enraged her.

"Motherfucker!" he said, laughing. "Motherfucker!"

She screamed, seething with anger and fighting against her restraints. The more she struggled, though, the more he laughed, and before long, she wore herself out, her shouting turning back to sobs.

A moment later, Mustafa went into one of the huts, still laughing, and closed the door behind him.

Wahab returned to the camp in the late morning, just before the sun reached its apex. Marah was just as glad to see him as she would have been to see Eden; even with Flaco around, Mustafa did whatever he wanted, but at least with Wahab present, he acted with some restraint.

Midday came and went, but Eden and Abu Tuan didn't return. Marah listened for Abu Tuan's call with a mixture of hope and fear, but she only heard the cheery music of the fruit doves, white-eyes, and bleeding-hearts. After rising from a nap, Mustafa emerged from one of the huts and issued an order in Tausug to Flaco. Flaco set out into the jungle with a machete, and Marah closed her eyes and tried to sleep. She couldn't stop seeing Mustafa in her mind, so she sat up and looked off into the jungle to distract herself. She watched a line of ginger ants streaming down the trunk of a rubber tree. Then she focused on the splatter of some bird droppings across a broad taro leaf.

After a while, Flaco returned from the jungle, carrying two squirming monitor lizards by the tails. He smashed their heads against a tree, gutted and skinned them, and then roasted them over the fire. Marah watched as Flaco gave the livers and tails to the others and took the less desirable parts for himself. She watched as he chewed the tough meat off the tiny bones, taking note of his jealousy and resentment toward the others, especially Mustafa.

After the men finished eating, Flaco cleaned up after them, and Mustafa rolled a thick blunt. Seeing an opportunity, Marah spoke.

"I have to go to the bathroom," she said.

The men ignored her, passing around the joint.

"Come on," she said. "I really have to go."

Flaco looked over, but the others continued to pay her no mind.

"Please," she said. "It's been all day."

After a moment, Mustafa issued an order in Tausug to Flaco and tossed him a set of keys. Flaco grabbed his FAL 7.62, approached Marah, and uncuffed her from the tree. He helped her to her feet and chained her hands in front of her.

Then he nudged her toward the jungle.

They wound their way through the wilderness. An animal squawked high up in the trees above them; it sounded like a drunken woman cackling.

Once she knew they were out of earshot from the camp, Marah turned and spoke to Flaco.

"You like Jay-Z?" she said.

Flaco didn't reply. She nodded to his T-shirt.

"You know," she said. "Jay-Z?"

Judging by his expression, he didn't seem to understand.

"You speak English?" she asked.

He muttered something in Spanish-sounding Chabacano and pushed her onward, and after a moment, she turned back to face him again.

"*Habla español?*" she said.

A look of surprise flashed across his face. Sensing an opening, she continued, speaking to him in a crude and rusty Spanish.

"I took some Spanish in high school," she said. "My name's Marah. And you are . . . ?"

He said nothing. After a moment, she went ahead and spoke, answering her own question.

"It's Flaco, right?" she said, turning back again to face him.

He stopped for a moment, startled, before prodding her onward with the FAL 7.62. Marah turned around and looked ahead again. She carefully considered her next words, knowing it might be the only opportunity she'd get to plead their case. *What is the Spanish word for "outcome"?* she wondered. *Consecuencia? Salida?* She couldn't remember. She didn't want to come off sounding harsh, but she didn't want to sound like she was begging, either.

She turned around and spoke again in her clunky Spanish.

"You know New York City?" asked Marah.

He didn't respond.

"That's okay," she said. "You don't have to talk."

Flaco finally responded in his thick, Chabacano dialect of Spanish, nudging her on with the tip of his machine gun.

"Keep moving," he said.

Sensing another opening, Marah continued.

"I had some Filipino neighbors," said Marah. "Chris and Ireez. There's lots of Filipinos in New York City."

He tried to ignore her as they picked their way through the jungle, and before long, they reached the small clearing with the murky stream.

"Stop here," said Flaco.

Marah turned around to face him. "This doesn't have to end badly for you," she replied in her halting Spanish.

Ignoring her, he unlocked her handcuffs and nudged her toward the stream. "Go on," he said in Chabacano, turning aside.

Marah approached the stream and squatted next to it. "You know how this will turn out," she said in Spanish. "You must hear things on the news—"

Flaco interrupted her, glancing around and visibly uncomfortable. "Hurry up," he said.

"These things always end badly," she said.

"You don't know what you're talking about," said Flaco, finally engaging with her.

Rather than backing off, she kept at him, her Spanish improving as her confidence increased. "Even if my stepfather comes through with the money, which is a big 'if,' it won't be a tenth of what you're asking for, and the

...ilitary will hunt you down before you even spend a cent," she said.

Flaco said nothing, but it was clear from his jumpy eyes and sideways glances that she was beginning to get to him.

"It's not too late," she said, emboldened, pulling up her shorts and approaching him. "I can help you. You're what, fourteen? Fifteen? Maybe I can even help get you to the US."

"I'm not interested."

"Those guys aren't your friends," she said. "Look at the way they treat you. They make you do all the work, and they barely give you anything to eat. That guy beat the hell out of you for not getting coconuts fast enough—"

"You don't know what you're talking about," snapped Flaco, finally turning to face her.

"I'm trying to help you," said Marah. "I mean really help you."

Flaco didn't say anything. His eyes glassed over, and for a moment, it looked like he might be choking up.

"You know, the military is probably on their way here as we speak," said Marah in her broken Spanish. "For all you know, they already captured your friend. He might even be telling them where we are right now—"

A loud and angry voice interrupted Marah from the jungle.

"The fuck?"

She and Flaco turned to see Mustafa approaching, his M16 strapped over his shoulder. Flaco began to speak, but before he could finish, Mustafa smashed the stock of his rifle across Flaco's face, dropping him.

Marah spoke. "Wait—"

Ignoring her, Mustafa kicked Flaco in the stomach and the ribs. Marah grabbed Mustafa by the arm.

"Stop it!" she cried.

He shoved her away, then resumed pummeling Flaco, kicking him until he stopped moving and then kicking him again for good measure. Then he turned and grabbed Marah by the neck.

"Talk to him again and you're dead," he said. "Understand?"

She hesitated, recoiling in his grip. He yanked her head back by her hair and brought his face so close to hers that she could smell his rank, gamy breath and see the decay of his teeth.

"Do you understand?" he repeated.

She nodded, trembling. "Y-yes."

He shoved her back in the direction of the camp. "Move."

Marah stumbled off into the jungle. After a few paces, she turned and looked back at the clearing. Flaco lay there on the ground, motionless and bleeding from his nose, ear, and mouth.

CHAPTER SIXTEEN

The afternoon gave way to another night. The sun disappeared behind the awning of trees, taking the heat along with it. The earthy, pungent smells of the jungle as it baked during the day were replaced again by the nighttime scents of salt, mold, and rotting jackfruit. Luzon rails and band-bellied crakes chattered in the distance, and one by one, the other birds, animals, and insects joined in, recommencing their frenzied nocturne.

Just before dark, Marah watched as Mustafa got a bamboo bow and a quiver of cane arrows from one of the huts. He then set off into the jungle, leaving his machine gun behind. After Mustafa was gone, Flaco stood from where he was resting, his right eye blackened and his nose swollen to the size of a lime. He approached the fire, cradling his sore ribs, and threw a split log atop the ashes, then returned to his place in the shadows.

Over by the huts, Wahab smoked a hand-rolled cigarette while reading an old section of newspaper. Marah tried to see where the newspaper was from, hoping she might determine their location. She frowned when she saw it was a copy of the *Mindanao Times*, which covered the entire Mindanao island group. There were over a thousand islands in the chain, which covered forty thousand square miles; for all she knew, they could have been close to the Visayas, Semporna, the Negros Islands, or even Northern Sulawesi.

She thought about Eden, wondering if he was having better luck than she'd had. He was a great convincer, a skill she'd reluctantly admired; she'd seen him negotiate a well-below-market deal on a West Side apartment for them, and she regularly overheard him talking clients into deals they'd been reluctant to make. He could talk her into almost anything as well, and often did, from going skydiving to taking ecstasy on a trip to Bali to shifting half of their savings into a tech startup. *But what can he say to my stepfather that I haven't already said?* she wondered. *And will my stepfather actually listen to him?* Though she'd never gotten the sense that her stepfather disliked Eden, Eden's cockiness had always seemed to rub Tom the wrong way.

Growing queasy, Marah looked up and studied the

passing clouds. After the last traces of sunlight bled from the jungle, Mustafa returned to the clearing, carrying what looked like a cross between a skunk and a ferret. Once he gutted and skinned the animal, he skewered it on a piece of green cane and set it by the fire, then went back into the forest with a plastic bucket. A few minutes later, he returned with a bucketful of fiddleheads, which he used to make some sort of stew while the cloud rat finished roasting.

As ugly as the animal had looked while alive, it smelled incredible to Marah while it cooked, reminding her of Thanksgiving dinners at her grandparents' home. Once the cloud rat was ready to eat, Mustafa took it off the fire and tore it in two. He kept the larger half for himself and gave the smaller half to Wahab, who then tore off the head and snout and tossed it to Flaco. The men ate the cloud rat with dirty cups of the fiddlehead stew, sucking the tiny bones of the animal clean before spitting them into the fire.

They didn't share anything with Marah, and after her previous pleas had fallen on deaf ears, she didn't bother asking them, either.

The stars burned like tracer fire in a clear and cloudless sky. Orion stood overhead with his club raised in an eternal standoff against Taurus, and off to the west, Zeus disguised himself as a swan.

Marah knelt against the tree, unable to sleep. She fought off the onslaught of insects while trying to think of a plan, but nothing came to mind, other than strategies that seemed suicidal, cowardly, or both. At one point, she thought she heard a plane engine in the distance, but when she looked up, she saw nothing, and the sound quickly faded away. At another point, she could've sworn she'd heard a woman shouting in the jungle, but the shouting soon became high-pitched and trilling, and she'd realized it was just another bird.

Before long, she heard the familiar call that was being used by the men. Wahab rose from where he was sitting at the fire and responded with the same call, and Mustafa emerged from one of the huts. A moment later, Eden stumbled into camp, bleeding from the mouth and a gash above one eye, his wrists bound behind him. Abu Tuan followed, shoving Eden along every few paces.

Marah watched as Wahab and Mustafa dragged Eden over to the rubber trees. They pushed him to the ground and cuffed him to the tree before joining Abu Tuan and Flaco over by the fire. Marah spoke as soon as the men were gone.

"What happened?" she asked.

"They got in an argument," he said, spitting out a

mouthful of blood. "I tried to escape—"

"What?"

"It was suicide, I know, but if we don't get that money we're fucked—"

"Shut up!" Abu Tuan shouted at them from the fire.

They stopped talking and waited for the men to ignore them before resuming their conversation.

"What were they arguing about?" said Marah.

"I don't know," said Eden. "These guys brought down their demands, but your stepfather won't budge."

"Maybe they just don't have it in cash."

"They can get it, though, can't they?" he said. "I mean, they must have access. Their properties alone are worth millions—"

Mustafa stormed over from the fire.

"I told you to shut up," he said.

"Wait—"

Before Eden could finish, Mustafa grabbed him by the hair and smashed his head against the tree.

"Eden!" screamed Marah.

The others rushed over as Mustafa smashed Eden's head against the tree, again and again. Marah's screaming turned to sobbing when they finally managed to pull Mustafa away.

CHAPTER SEVENTEEN

Marah gazed up at the stars, lost in thought. She recalled the summer nights when her grandfather had taught her how to navigate using the constellations. The hot blue Pleiades were easy to spot and helpful for getting one's bearings, and Cassiopeia was helpful in finding the North Star, which in turn made for a great fixed point for drawing measurements.

Her thoughts drifted toward her late father. *What would he have done, if he were in her stepfather's position?* Her father had always been a rock, strong and calm, and she'd never doubted him. Her stepfather was a different subject, though; he wasn't a bad or weak person, but she didn't have the same faith in him, and not just because he wasn't blood-related, either. *And what about her mother? Why isn't she doing more?* She wondered what she'd do in her mother's situation, if it had been her on the other end of the line. Hell, she'd give everything she had just to have a child, much less to save one she'd already had. *Is her mother just going along with her stepfather, or is she trying to get the money? Do they really not have the money, or are they getting advised not to give in?* She wasn't so sure.

She went around and around in her head, her corkscrewing thoughts driving her further and further into a pit of despair. She soon felt her airways constricting again, and she found herself struggling to breathe, gasping in short, ragged breaths. She looked over at Eden, who slumped motionless against the tree he was handcuffed to. For a moment, she worried that he might be dead, but then he shifted in sleep, groaning.

A moment later, one of the men cleared his throat over by the fire. Somewhere in the distance, a bird cried out, and another bird shrieked in response before the silence returned.

Marah spent the morning watching the men. They did their chores without communicating, aside from the occasional grunted command from Mustafa to Flaco or Wahab. Abu Tuan went back into his hut after breakfast and remained there until what Marah guessed to be about noon, judging by the location of the sun. Then he emerged with a sack in one hand and a pair of rusty handcuffs in the other, and he approached her, dropping the handcuffs at her feet.

"Put them on," he said.

They made their way through the jungle, heading back in the direction of the beach. The canopy of trees shielded them from the midday sun, and a salt-tinged breeze blew past them, taking some of the heat along with it.

After a while, the rain began to fall. Marah heard a soft tapping somewhere off to her left, then more patter behind her, and then a louder drumming to her right and ahead of them, and before she knew it, they were caught in a downpour. What didn't directly reach them pooled and collected on broad leaves and soon hit them in splashes and streams, and within seconds, they were soaked, their clothes sticking to their skin.

Abu Tuan shoved her onward through the jungle, and they soon made it to the beach. Once they were out in the open, Marah looked up toward the sky and spotted some slow-moving cloud masses to the south, their dark tendrils trailing behind them. They looked oddly comical to her, like a group of manatees rutting in slow motion.

They walked out into the ocean and trudged their

way toward the anchored boat. The deeper that Marah went, the more the rain seemed to be coming from beneath them and to their sides just as much as it was coming from above. If she closed her eyes, it sounded like frying bacon, a sound that recalled lazy Sunday mornings when she and Eden were first together, when she'd wake to the sounds of him making her breakfast after a late night out. It had been years since they'd gone out all night; they'd stopped going out late in their early thirties, around the time she'd begun trying to get pregnant, and the late breakfasts and all the other little things they once did for each other had slowly fallen by the wayside as well. She felt strangely nostalgic for those days, even though at the time, she couldn't wait for the next phase of her life. Her reminiscing didn't last long, though—a wave crashed over her and nearly swept her under.

Abu Tuan grabbed her by the back of the shirt and shoved her onward. Before long, he reached the boat and pulled himself aboard, then pulled up Marah and pushed her toward the hull.

"Get down," he said.

She dropped to a knee, bent forward, and lowered herself. Then Abu Tuan unfurled the tarp over her and started up the boat's engines. Marah counted to herself again as they raced across the ocean. *One, two, three, four . . . tap, tap, tap-tap-tap-tap-tap.* The sound of the rain hitting the tarp merged with the roar of the boat engines, drowning out her internal counting.

Sometime after reaching a count of two thousand, Marah fell into a light and dreamless asleep.

"Get up," said Abu Tuan, pulling the tarp off Marah.

She snapped awake, startled. Then she opened her eyes and glanced around. They were tied to a dock somewhere; other than a few lilting palm trees and a trash-strewn coastline, there were no other indicators of their location. The sky was overcast and gray, covering the sun like a thick cataract.

Abu Tuan pushed Marah onto the dock, and they made their way onto the beach. They walked up the coast a ways and toward a path that wound through the sparse jungle. At the end of the path, Marah spotted a rusty sedan parked by the shoulder of the cul-de-sac. Abu Tuan unlocked the sedan's trunk and turned to face her.

"Get in," he said.

She did, and he closed the trunk lid over her. As Abu Tuan started up the car and drove off, Marah started counting again while she rode in the trunk. With the clouds blocking most of the sunlight, it was much cooler than the other rides had been, and she hardly even broke a sweat. Before long, the ride went from bumpy to smooth.

They finally began to slow after Marah reached a count of twenty-eight hundred. At twenty-nine hundred, they stopped for a moment before making a left-hand turn, and just before she reached thirty-one hundred, they turned right. They made one more right-hand turn when Marah reached a count of thirty-two hundred. Then the car came to a stop, and she heard the engine shut off.

Marah heard a car door open. She heard footsteps approaching on what sounded like pavement. The trunk lid opened, and Marah saw Abu Tuan standing there, holding a plastic bag. He grabbed her by the arm and pulled her out of the trunk. She glanced at her surroundings; they were in an alley behind a run-down concrete building.

Abu Tuan fanned open his balisong and cut the zip tie binding Marah's wrists. Then he pulled the abaya and hijab from the plastic bag and handed them to her.

"Wear these," he said.

She did as she was told and followed Abu Tuan around to the other side of the building.

Once there, she spotted a grubby port city in the distance.

They walked toward the city center, passing an old Chinese cemetery that took up most of a valley. The hills were studded with ornately carved graves and charnel houses that backed right up into the earth. The farther up into the hills, the more overgrown the jungle became, and it made it difficult to tell where the graveyard ended and where the jungle began.

After passing a number of signs and buildings on the outskirts of the city, Marah realized that they were approaching Sandakan. She'd heard of the city before; it had been the capital of British North Borneo, and most of the island's palm oil and cocoa left from its port. It had also been the location of a POW labor camp during World War II—as a girl, she'd been fascinated with the war; both of her grandfathers had fought in it—and she knew it had been the departure point for the Sandakan Death Marches. She remembered a photograph she'd seen of its few survivors; the Allied soldiers had looked like the prisoners at Auschwitz and Dachau, with hollow eyes, sunken chests, and ribs that showed through their skin.

They approached a few blocks of dilapidated buildings crammed between a dirty waterfront and a steep ridge overlooking the bay. The majority of the people Marah saw there were Chinese; she didn't see a single Westerner among them.

Abu Tuan spotted a phone booth and pushed Marah toward it, but before they could reach it, he grabbed her arm and stopped walking.

"Wait," he said.

She stopped and looked in the direction that he was looking, spotting a muscular, white Westerner with a buzz cut and aviator sunglasses standing by an SUV that was covered with mud.

"What?" she asked.

He didn't reply. She saw another shorthaired Westerner emerge from a small shop and approach the SUV.

"Turn around," said Abu Tuan.

Before she could react, he shoved her back in the direction that they'd come from.

CHAPTER EIGHTEEN

The boat sped across the ocean, flying from one crest to the next. It skipped across the water like a cast stone, leaving no trace behind.

Marah lay in the hull, cradling her head with her zip-tied hands. Abu Tuan seemed to be in a hurry to get back to the island, pushing the boat even faster than before. She was thrown from one side of the boat to the other and then back again, barely able to protect herself. She tried counting for a while but could hardly concentrate, so she eventually just gave up.

She thought about the Westerners they'd seen, and why they'd alarmed Abu Tuan. *Are they US military? Special ops?* It seemed unlikely; the US military rarely got involved with kidnapping cases, unless their interests were at stake. *Or are they contractors or negotiators in the ransom trade? Would her stepfather have hired someone?* She wasn't sure.

Before she could think any further, they crashed down hard into a trough. Marah's head slammed against the hull with an audible crack, knocking her senseless, and for a moment, she even forgot where she was.

The rain had stopped falling, but the jungle was still wet. The leaves and trees were slick with rainwater, and the runoff had collected in pools and puddles on the softened jungle floor.

Abu Tuan shoved Marah through the jungle, back in the direction of their camp. Her head ached from getting tossed around in the boat, and she could still taste blood from repeatedly biting her tongue.

She stumbled on a downhill stretch and nearly lost her footing. Her pace didn't seem quick enough for Abu Tuan, so he kicked her in the back. She pitched forward, and, unable to use her zip-tied hands to block her fall, she landed face-first in the muck. She briefly thought about lying there, and about giving up. An image of her emaciated father in his hospital bed popped into her mind, causing her to shudder. *He'd never given up,* she'd remembered, *even when he'd dropped to 110 pounds and it had taken everything he'd had left just to utter a single syllable.*

"Get up," said Abu Tuan, yanking her back to her feet.

Marah gritted her teeth and struggled onward.

They reached the camp as the sun began its slow lilt toward the horizon. Eden seemed to perk up when he saw Marah, in better spirits than he'd been before. Hearing their return, Mustafa emerged from one of the huts, shirtless; his bleary, red eyes widened when he saw them, and he said something to the others in Tausug.

Abu Tuan handcuffed Marah back to the tree before joining the others.

"What happened?" asked Eden.

"He got spooked by something," said Marah, watching as the men got into a heated discussion in Tausug over by the fire.

"What?"

"There were some Westerners there."

"You mean like tourists?"

"No," she said. "I mean official-looking. Like government, security, that sort of thing."

"You think your parents told someone?"

"I don't know—"

Before she could finish, Mustafa grabbed a machine

gun and stormed toward them, shouting in Tausug. He put the tip of the machine gun against Eden's head, spitting what sounded like curses at him.

"Wait!" said Eden, closing his eyes.

Abu Tuan and Wahab pulled Mustafa away from Eden before he could shoot. Then Abu Tuan turned and shouted something in Tausug to Flaco. Flaco disappeared into a hut while Mustafa continued to rail at the others. He returned a moment later with two coils of rope and two canvas drawstring bags, which he brought to Abu Tuan.

"What are you doing?" said Marah, trying vainly to back away.

Abu Tuan said nothing, uncuffing Eden and shoving him to the ground. Wahab then hog-tied Eden, tying his hands behind his back, then tying his elbows together, and then his ankles, finishing it off by tying it all together.

"You son of a bitch," said Eden, struggling against his restraints.

They uncuffed Marah from the tree and started hog-tying her as well.

"Let go of me—" she began.

"Shut up," said Abu Tuan.

He put one of the canvas bags over Eden's head and pulled the drawstrings tight.

"Wait, don't—"

Before Marah could finish, Wahab put the other bag

over her head and pulled it tight, and the world went black. Marah began sucking for air in deep gulps. As she inhaled, she drew the bag into her mouth, and she could taste something coppery and salty on the fabric. At first, she thought the bag might've been used to carry meat.

Then she realized with horror that it was dried blood.

CHAPTER NINETEEN

Marah began to hyperventilate. The quicker her breathing became, the less air she was able to take in, and the less air she took in, the quicker her breathing became. It was a vicious cycle, and she soon began to feel like she was drowning. She tried to recite the prayers she knew in order to slow her breathing—the Lord's Prayer and the St. Francis Prayer, which her Aunt Helen had had on the wall of her Chappaqua home—but they didn't help. She tried four-count breathing, too, but it didn't work, either. She even tried the Dickinson poem again, but her throat continued to tighten until it felt like she was sucking through a coffee straw. *Who was she kidding?* she thought to herself. *Hope wasn't a thing with feathers; it was a farce, an empty salve that did nothing to deter the inevitable.*

Her thoughts drifted back toward her failed attempts to appeal to Flaco. Then she thought about the moment she got into their captors' boat, and the moment back in Shanghai when she agreed to go on the vacation in the first place. *If only she'd done things differently*, she rationalized, *then perhaps she wouldn't be lying there, hooded and hog-tied on the ground.* She went around and around in her head, cursing herself and second-guessing her every move.

She racked her brain, trying to think of some possible way to escape. Perhaps she could find something to cut through her restraints; maybe a sharp rock, she figured, or a piece of metal. She couldn't move, though, and there'd been no sharp rocks or anything else lying around the camp. *And even if I was able to find something to cut through my restraints*, she wondered, *what then? Would I really be able to take on the men?* It seemed unlikely for even the broadest of Hollywood screenplays.

The more she thought about it, the more she began to feel another anxiety attack coming on. She felt nauseous and weak, and her heart raced. She put aside thoughts of escape and thought instead about the kite fliers at Century Park in Shanghai, the old master sketches at the Met, and other things that she enjoyed. Before long, though, she gave up, ashamed, knowing they were just distractions and wouldn't change the situation.

She looked back over her life and cursed herself for all the time she'd wasted stressing over things that either weren't meant to be or things that had never come. She regretted not having taken more risks, like Eden had. *What has playing it safe ever gotten me, anyway?* she wondered. Maybe if she hadn't tried so hard, things would've turned out the same, or perhaps even better. Maybe she would've even given birth; that had been the case with her friend, Sydney. Sydney had spent years trying to conceive, only to give up trying and instead adopt a Chinese girl, but before the adopted girl had even turned one, Sydney had gotten pregnant and ended up having a child the following year. Maybe stressing over everything had actually only made things worse, for all she knew.

She started to cry. She'd spent so much time analyzing and worrying about everything, and now that her life appeared to be drawing to a close, she would've given everything she had to go back and do it over differently, and more fearlessly. She recalled a Dylan Thomas poem she'd read during her freshman year; her teacher had brought an old vinyl record into class of Thomas himself reading the lines. She could practically hear them in her head, in that baritone, whiskey-soaked voice. She could hear the words again as if it was only yesterday that she was hearing them for the first time, and their meaning finally seemed to come to her now. Their true meaning. Not just some textbook, intellectual understanding but something experiential and firsthand, decades later and thousands of miles away from that classroom. If she had another chance to do it all over, she would have raged more; she would have stood up more. She would have taken more risks and worried less about the outcomes. She knew that wishing for this was pointless, though; she might as well be wishing for wings to sprout from her back. There was no going back; life had no reset button, and there was only one direction — forward, ever forward — and there didn't seem to be that far to go.

Her despair soon became anger, first at her captors, and then at Eden for getting them into the situation in the first place. Then the anger turned inward, cutting her down like a scythe. The vacation wasn't his fault; it was hers — he was trying to help her, and to pull her out of her depression. He hadn't pulled away from her; she'd pulled away from him and had gone inward in the first place. She was just as responsible for everything as he was, if not more so.

Sick of thinking about it, she began to struggle. She gnashed her teeth, bit at the hood, and head-butted the ground. She rocked back and forth and strained to push herself off the ground. She shouted as loud as she could and fought against her restraints until her wrists and ankles bled and her forehead hurt and she could barely breathe, but nothing answered her. Nothing came back from the other side.

No matter what she did, no one out there seemed to be able to hear her, or if they did hear her, they didn't seem to care.

At some point in the middle of the night, Marah started to fall in and out of a light sleep. She eventually nodded off, and before long, she dreamed that she and Eden were riding bicycles through Central Park, back when they were living in New York City. They stopped to order drinks at an outdoor café, and while waiting for them, she reached forward to put her arms around Eden. Before she could embrace him, though, he vanished. She spun around and saw her father standing behind her, wearing the same clothes that Eden had been wearing, and when she reached for him, he also disappeared.

Marah opened her mouth to speak, but before she could, she heard someone shouting nearby in Tausug. Then she heard someone else shouting in Tausug. She opened her eyes but saw nothing; she felt the rough canvas against her face, and smelled the dried blood, and she remembered that she was wearing a hood.

She started to panic again, gasping for air and

sucking the canvas bag into her mouth. Unable to slow her breathing or distract herself, she decided instead to immerse herself in the moment, picking out the sounds of the jungle the way that Eden had taught her to pick out the sounds of individual instruments while listening to jazz. He'd taken her to see a show at the Iridium on one of their first dates. She'd never been a fan of jazz; it had always sounded so freewheeling and cacophonic to her, as opposed to the more controlled arrangements of Tori Amos, Ben Harper, and other artists she preferred. After he showed her how to actively listen to the music, though, she developed an appreciation for it, and for the way Thelonious Monk could lead a band with his dissonant harmonies and percussive attacks, or how John Coltrane's improvisations could work within a piece while also rising above it. She identified the individual sounds in the discord around her: here was the whoop of a gibbon, and the sound of bending branches as it made its way through the forest canopy. There was the shriek of a minivet and the croaking of some sort of toad.

The sounds of the jungle night soon gave way to the music of its dawn. Marah heard the chattering macaques. She heard the loud and aggressive hooting of a male trogon, and she heard a foraging wild boar crashing through the dense underbrush. Eventually, she began to hear the men rising. She heard one of them walk to the edge of the clearing and urinate against some trees. She heard another fill the pot with water from a jug. Then she heard some discussion in Tausug between what sounded like Abu Tuan and Wahab. She painted the scene in her mind: the nocturnal creatures were returning to their lairs, the ants and bees were busy at work, and the sun was baking off the white mist that had shrouded the jungle.

She heard someone say something again in Tausug. Then she heard approaching footsteps and felt someone grab her arm. Before she could figure out what was happening, someone yanked her to her feet. Then someone else pulled the hood off her head.

The harsh sunlight blinded Marah. She squinted around as she stood unsteadily in the mud, struggling to get her bearings. Things slowly came into focus — she saw Eden nearby, hooded and hog-tied on the ground; she saw Abu Tuan standing next to her, holding her arm; she saw Flaco across from her, gripping his FAL 7.62 with both hands, sunlight glinting off its barrel. The men all looked nervous and expectant, like something had happened or something was about to happen. It was difficult to tell what time it was; it could have been nine or ten in the morning, or it could have been early in the afternoon.

Eden's muffled voice finally broke the silence. "Marah?"

"I'm here," she said.

"What's happening?"

"I don't know—"

Before she could finish, Abu Tuan pushed her toward the jungle.

"Move," he said.

"They're taking me away again," said Marah.

"You have to get the money—"

Mustafa interrupted him. "Shut up."

"If you don't get it, we're gonna die out here—"

Mustafa kicked Eden in the ribs.

"Eden—"

Before Marah could finish, Abu Tuan shoved her into the jungle.

CHAPTER TWENTY

Somewhere in the distance, a barbet cried out. At first, its call was buried underneath the grinding of the cicadas and the mosquitoes. Before long, it emerged from the noise. Then it faded back into the background again, swallowed once more by the dense jungle soundscape.

Marah and Abu Tuan made their way back toward the beach. He shoved and kicked her along, showing less patience and restraint than he'd shown her before. Even though it was early, she was already exhausted; her back ached from the position she'd slept in, and nearly every inch of her was covered with insect bites, rashes, and sunburn. She felt sick to her stomach, and she couldn't stop thinking about Eden; she kept picturing Mustafa kicking him in the ribs, again and again.

They passed the massive tipolo tree, then slid their way down the hills and through the muck. Marah stumbled while crossing the river and fell to the rocks. Abu Tuan yanked her back to her feet, and they continued on, soon reaching the beach.

After emerging from the jungle, they trudged across the hot sand and entered the water. Once again, it felt incredible to Marah, as good as anything she'd ever felt in her life. The thought of going under and letting the current take her away crossed her mind. Then she thought of Eden back at the clearing, and she gritted her teeth and trudged onward.

They waded out toward the boat. Abu Tuan climbed aboard first and then pulled Marah aboard after him. He shoved Marah toward the center of the boat, then grabbed her by the back of the neck and pushed her down onto her knees. After she lay down on her side, he unfurled the tarp over her. Then he started the boat's engines.

A moment later, Abu Tuan swung the boat around and began to head away from the island. Before long, Marah started to hyperventilate again. She closed her eyes. She wanted to surrender; she just wanted it to be over. *If the men want to kill us, so be it,* she figured. She just wanted it to be quick, and for the pain to end. Then she heard her father's calm and steady voice inside her head. *Don't give up,* it said. *Don't quit five minutes before the miracle.* As a child, she'd always hated his sayings; she'd thought they were such clichés, so fraudulent and shopworn. Now, his words felt like oases in a vast desert.

She murmured her father's words under her breath, over and over again, and then resumed reciting the Dickinson poem. Before reaching its end, though, she gave up, breaking down in tears.

They bounded across the sea in the flimsy craft, sailing from one crest to the next or occasionally slamming down hard into a trough. Marah bounced about the hull, counting in her head while trying to avoid injury. Just after she reached a count of fifty-six hundred, the roar of the engines diminished, and the boat began to slow. After it felt like the boat was dragged ashore, Abu Tuan pulled the tarp off Marah.

"Get up," he said.

Marah sat up, and Abu Tuan pulled her to her feet. She glanced around at their surroundings; there were no docks, and a flotsam of tires, plastic bottles, and other garbage littered the shoreline. It was clearly a different location than the one they'd arrived at before.

Abu Tuan pushed Marah off the boat. She stepped onto the wet sand, and Abu Tuan pulled an old pair of black jellies from a plastic bag and dropped them at her feet.

"Put them on," he said.

They smelled like rancid milk, and their moist insides squished when she stepped into them, but she was grateful to have something covering her feet.

He nudged Marah inland. They walked up the beach and toward a narrow path, then made their way through a sparse jungle. Marah looked for clues regarding their location, but there weren't any to be found, other than sappanwood trees, spotted mangroves, and other beach and scrub vegetation. It could have been Malaysia or the Philippines; for all she knew, it could've even been Indonesia.

At the end of the path, Marah spotted a Toyota Tamaraw MPV parked on the shoulder of a dirt road. Rust-eaten and covered with dents, it looked like a rotting piece of fruit. She checked it for identifying marks, but it had none, other than a mud-splattered, black-and-white license plate.

Abu Tuan approached the MPV and opened its rear door, then turned to Marah.

"Get in," he said.

Marah counted again while she rode in the back of the MPV. Abu Tuan had put a hood over her head and had covered her with a blanket, so it was even hotter than it had been when she'd ridden in the trunk. The blanket smelled like mold and rotten meat, and it was made of a rough material that irritated her skin. At one point, the MPV hit a pothole, and her head slammed against the wheel well; at another point, she bit her tongue when they ran over some debris.

After a while, the ride went from bumpy to smooth. They began to slow after Marah had reached a count of eight hundred. At nine hundred, they stopped for a moment before making a left-hand turn, and just before she reached a thousand, they turned right.

They made one more right-hand turn when Marah reached a count of twelve hundred. Then the car came to a stop, and she heard the engine shut off. Marah heard a car door open. She heard footsteps approaching, but it didn't sound like asphalt or loose gravel this time; it sounded like mud. The rear door opened, and Abu Tuan took the blanket and hood off Marah and yanked her to her feet. Then she squinted at her surroundings.

The MPV stood on the shoulder of a dirt road, and in the distance, Marah could see the outskirts of a shantytown.

CHAPTER TWENTY-ONE

Dense barrios built upon stilts littered the coastline.
Children collected water in gasoline cans at the shore, and
a scattering of locals congregated at an open-air market.

Abu Tuan shoved Marah toward the shantytown,
avoiding the congested areas. Wearing the abaya and
hijab, she was once again invisible. She looked inland,
where volcanic mountains rose steeply from the
overgrown jungle. The island itself seemed to be born
from violence and fire, which somehow didn't come as a
surprise to her; there were clues to its turbulent history
everywhere she looked, in its jagged landscape, its
hardscrabble vegetation, and its sinewy people.

They made their way through the barangay. It was
different from the other towns they'd visited; the people

were mostly Tausug, and Marah overheard them speaking the same choppy, Arabic-sounding language as the men. She glanced around for clues to their location. There weren't many; it was little more than a shantytown, but among the locals weaving mats or selling lanzones and jackfruit, she saw a few signs in Arabic and an occasional Filipino flag.

Abu Tuan led Marah into an open hut made from warped boards and corrugated metal siding. It had a packed dirt floor, and there were no furnishings other than a pair of wooden cable spools and an empty crate. He reached into a canvas sack and pulled out a handful of cheap cell phones, selecting one and dialing a number on it. He then covered the cell's microphone with his hand and turned to Marah.

"Last chance," he said. "Make it count."

Marah took the phone from Abu Tuan and raised it to her ear.

"Hello?" she said.

Her stepfather answered at the other end of the line. "Marah? Are you okay?"

She opened her mouth to speak out of reflex. Then she hesitated for a moment. Abu Tuan nudged her, impatient.

"Go on," he said.

After a moment, Marah calmly spoke.

"Put my mother on," she said.

"Marah—"

She interrupted him.

"Put her on."

After another moment, she heard her mother's voice.

"Honey?"

Marah hesitated for a moment, startled by the shaky timbre of her mother's voice. It suddenly dawned on Marah why she was so often angry with her mother—she was just like her, fragile and full of fear, the antithesis of what her father had been and of what she'd always wanted to be. Marah's anger began to fade, replaced by a sense of love and compassion, and not only for her mother but also for herself.

After a long moment, Marah finally spoke. "I love you," she said.

"Marah . . ."

Her mother's voice broke. Even though she couldn't see her mother, she knew that her mother was crying.

"It's okay," said Marah, beginning to cry herself.

"I love you, too," said her mother.

"I know," said Marah, smiling.

Abu Tuan yanked the phone and spoke into the receiver. "You have twenty-four hours."

Without waiting for a reply, he hung up and dropped the phone back into the sack.

Marah turned away and spotted a reedy toddler playing in the dirt nearby. The child's bubbling laughter seemed so surreal and out of place.

They walked back through the barangay and made their way to the MPV. After Marah took off the hijab and abaya, Abu Tuan bound her wrists with a zip tie, pulling so tightly that it bit into her flesh. She climbed into the back of the vehicle without even being asked, and he put the hood back over her head. Then he closed the door behind her.

After a moment, Marah heard the engine starting, then felt the vehicle slowly turning around. She began counting again, but she gave up before even reaching a count of ten.

She resumed reciting the Dickinson poem. After finishing the poem, she recited it two more times. Then she opened her eyes and started to count again. By the time she got to a hundred, her breathing finally started to slow down.

When she reached a count of three hundred, it was almost back to normal.

Marah and Abu Tuan trudged through the jungle back in

the direction of the coastline. Her pace seemed too slow for him, so he kicked her.

"Keep moving," he said.

She stumbled onward, and they soon reached the coast. The blazing sand looked blood red in the midday heat, and the sun was directly overhead. They made their way up the beach and entered the water, then waded out to the boat. Upon reaching it, Marah climbed into it and lay down in the hull. Abu Tuan followed her on board and unfurled the blue tarp over her, and after another moment, she heard him start the outboard motors.

She lay underneath the tarp, her hands bound before her. The motorboat eventually banked in a wide arc. During the turn, something rolled across the hull toward Marah's feet. She ignored it at first, but after it bumped against her feet again, she strained to look down. Her eyes widened when she saw a rusty screwdriver lying at her feet.

Marah hesitated for a moment, considering it. She heard a voice in her head, a loud and angry voice that said, *Don't bother.* She shook off the urge to try and get it— the voice was right, after all; what match was a rusty screwdriver against a machine gun? Then she heard another voice, a calmer, steadier voice that said, *What are you waiting for? Reach down and grab it . . . it's right there at your feet.*

After another long moment, Marah decided to act. She shifted around until she could grasp the screwdriver with her right foot. Then she struggled to bring it up to her hands. She dropped it before she could do so, though, and it quickly rolled away. Her heartbeat slowed, and in a way, she was relieved.

Marah could hear the loud, angry voice again in her head telling her to let it go. Before she could, though, the screwdriver rolled back toward her and bumped against her foot. Ignoring the loud voice in her head, Marah tried to grasp the screwdriver again with her right foot, and after a few unsuccessful attempts, she was able to bring it up to her hands. Feeling its cold plastic grip, she felt her heart thudding in her chest like a crazed bird trying to break free from its cage. She could hear Dylan Thomas's words echoing again in her mind.

Marah stuffed the screwdriver into the waistband of her shorts.

CHAPTER TWENTY-TWO

The sun began its descent toward the horizon. The wind had diminished during the afternoon, and the light boat flew across the placid sea.

Marah roasted under the tarp, the sweat gathering in her eyebrows. She tried keeping count, but she was too anxious to stay focused; the veins throbbed under her skin, and she couldn't stop her left foot from tapping. She resumed reciting the Dickinson poem, no longer trying to calm herself but rather steeling herself as if for battle. Each word and stanza added to the gathering momentum that built inside her.

The sound of the engines soon diminished, and the boat began to slow. The loud, angry voice gradually returned to Marah's thoughts. *Who are you kidding?* it told her. *Attacking him is suicide.* She shook the thoughts from her mind and took a deep breath, and the calmer, steadier voice eventually came back. *Doing nothing would be suicide,* it said. *You have to act, and the time to act is now.*

Abu Tuan killed the boat's engines, and a moment later, Marah heard the anchor splash as he tossed it overboard. Once the boat stopped drifting, Abu Tuan pulled back the tarp.

"Get up," he said.

She struggled to her feet, holding her zip-tied hands against the screwdriver so it wouldn't slide down her shorts. Then she approached the side of the boat, where Abu Tuan pushed her into the sea. Once in the water, she began to make her way toward shore. Abu Tuan dropped into the water after her and followed closely behind, carrying the machine gun over his head. At one point, Marah felt the screwdriver slipping down her inner thigh; she paused, pinching it between her legs, and then reached down to adjust it with her zip-tied hands.

"Keep moving," said Abu Tuan, shoving her onward.

She continued her way toward the shore, pressing her zip-tied hands against the screwdriver to keep it in place. She soon emerged from the water and made her way up the beachhead, and Abu Tuan stepped out of the ocean and followed her. Halfway to the jungle, Marah looked down and saw the outline of the screwdriver clearly visible through her wet shorts. Her heart skipped a beat; if Abu Tuan saw her from the front, he'd surely be able to see it. Her airways constricted, and she began having trouble breathing again. She knew she had to attack, and soon; waiting until they were in the jungle no longer seemed like an option.

With her back to him, Marah closed her eyes, took a deep breath, and slowly exhaled. Then she recited the final few lines of the Dickinson poem one last time before pulling the screwdriver from her waistband and getting a good grip on it. She paused at the slight incline at the jungle edge, letting Abu Tuan draw near.

"Go on," he said.

Just as he grabbed her by the shoulder, Marah spun around and plunged the screwdriver into his side, causing him to drop the M16. He grabbed her by her zip-tied wrists, groaning in pain and cursing at her in Tausug. She screamed, and they fell to the ground, wrestling for control of the screwdriver. The more they fought over it, the deeper it dug into Abu Tuan's side. He flipped Marah onto her back and pulled the pistol from his waistband, but she clumsily knocked it free with her bound hands. He punched her in the face, knocking her senseless for a moment, then reached for the screwdriver sticking out of his side, but before he could remove it, Marah grabbed him by the forearm and shoved the screwdriver in deeper, twisting it as hard as she could for good measure.

Abu Tuan head-butted Marah in the face, breaking her nose with a muffled thump; she saws stars and felt like she was drowning in a hot and coppery stew. He reached again for his side and managed to pull out the screwdriver, but he momentarily left himself open. Marah instinctively raised a knee into his crotch, and he dropped the screwdriver and rolled to his side, gasping for air. She crawled out from underneath him and reached for the fallen screwdriver, then turned over and swung it as hard as she could, piercing the center of his back. He reached for his back as if he'd been shot there, wheezing and sucking through a punctured lung, but he couldn't manage to grab the screwdriver. He struggled to his feet and staggered forward a few steps, gurgling and choking. Then he pitched forward and fell face-first to the sand. Marah scrambled to her feet, sucking for air. After a long moment, she struggled to pick up the pistol with her zip-tied hands, dropping it twice before managing to get a good grip on it. She then slowly approached Abu Tuan, unsteadily pointing the pistol at him. She kicked his foot, but he didn't move. She reached down with her zip-tied hands and touched the side of his neck, checking for a pulse, but she couldn't find one. Then she struggled to turn him over. He was much heavier than she'd expected him to be, and after a number of tries, she finally managed to roll him over and onto his back. He was clearly dead, and his empty, lifeless eyes stared blankly toward the sky.

Marah approached some jagged rocks and rubbed the zip tie against them until she cut through it, surprised at how quickly it came undone. Once her hands were free, she went back and rifled through Abu Tuan's pockets, finding the keys to the boat engine and a flip phone. She tried to dial a number on the phone, but the call didn't go through; there wasn't any reception. She shoved the phone and keys into her pocket, then grabbed Abu Tuan's machine gun and approached the jungle, but before she reached it, she stopped.

Then she turned around and went back for Abu Tuan's shoes.

CHAPTER TWENTY-THREE

Marah entered the jungle and soon found the trail. She
hurried along the narrow path as quietly as she could,
cradling the machine gun before her, her index finger
hovering above the trigger. The sounds of the coming
night filled the air all around her; there were grinding
cicadas and bellowing frogs, screeching hornbills and the
soft flapping of the giant jungle moths.

As she approached the camp, she felt her heartbeat
quickening. She wasn't feeling another anxiety attack
coming on, though; it was a new and different feeling. She
had a sense of awareness that was unfamiliar to her; she
felt totally present and attached to the moment. She wasn't
without fear, but she seemed to be without the panic that
had been plaguing her for so long. It was more of a feeling

of acceptance somehow; an acceptance of who she was and where she was, and of what had happened and what would happen, regardless of the outcome.

Marah crossed the stream, then went up the hill and passed the massive tipolo tree. She envisioned herself entering the camp, mowing down their captors like she was playing some first-person shooter video game. She felt light and loose, almost even giddy. It was like a powerful drunkenness, and the feeling grew and intensified with each additional step.

She continued through the jungle. Before long, she reached another stream she didn't remember having crossed. She hesitated, unsure; her newfound feelings of power and composure left her as quickly as they'd appeared, transforming back to the old, paralyzing senses of anxiety and dread.

A hornbill screeched in the distance, breaking Marah's reverie; it sounded like it was laughing at her. After a moment, she turned around and went back the way she'd come, changing directions when she reached the tipolo tree. Then she continued on her way, trudging up a slow-rising hill before scrambling down its other side.

She soon came to another creek and glanced around at her surroundings; once again, nothing looked familiar. Her spirits sank, and she felt a sob forming at the back of her throat. She stifled the urge to cry, pushing on across the creek and heading deeper into the jungle. She eventually spotted the tipolo tree again and realized she was going in circles.

Exasperated, she changed directions once more, only to find more unfamiliar territory. The thought suddenly occurred to her that her actions may have actually worsened their situation — that Eden might already be dead because of what she'd done, and that she'd soon be joining him. She felt the urge to throw up. She pulled out the cell phone and flipped it open, not even knowing who she'd call, or what anyone would've been able to do if she'd gotten through. It didn't matter, anyway; there was no reception. Putting away the cell phone, she could hear the loud, angry voice in her head saying, *I told you so. You should've listened, and now it's too late.* She felt another sob rising in her throat, and felt tears forming in her eyes. *Why am I such an idiot?* she asked herself. Then she heard the calmer, steadier voice, murmuring like a stream through a quiet forest. *Keep going*, it told her. *Just keep going.*

She continued on through the jungle and soon reached a creek, which she followed for a while. She glanced around, but again, nothing looked familiar. She pushed on until the creek met a stream, and then she followed the stream for a bit. Eventually, she began to recognize things: groups of trees she'd seen before or distant hills that she remembered.

She picked up her pace. Before long, she reached the area where their captors had taken them to relieve themselves. She changed directions and began to head back in the direction of the camp. Then she froze when she heard a branch snap nearby.

Marah ducked behind a copse of trees. She heard another branch break, then a wet, sucking noise, like a foot being pulled out of the muck. She squatted down and looked out at the stream through a small gap in the underbrush. Her heart skipped a beat when she spotted Wahab fetching a pail of water, his machine gun slung over his shoulder. Marah waited until Wahab finished filling the pail. When he turned and headed back in the direction of the camp, she began to follow him from a distance, staying far enough behind him so that he wouldn't hear her movements.

Wahab didn't seem to have any idea that he was being followed, so Marah began to cut the distance between them. Contrary to before, she felt stronger and calmer the closer she drew to him, rather than weaker and more terrified. She was no longer the pursued but now a pursuer; no longer a victim but in control of herself and her actions. When she accidently broke a branch, Marah stopped and raised her machine gun, expecting Wahab to spin around and fire upon her. But Wahab either didn't hear it or, if he did, he didn't react. Emboldened, Marah picked up her pace.

She cut the distance between them from forty feet to thirty, and then from thirty to twenty. Her breathing accelerated again as she drew closer to Wahab; the machine gun began to feel light and electric in her grip, jumping in her hands. She squeezed them tightly around the barrel and the stock, took in a deep breath, and let it out slowly. Her hands steadied again, and the machine gun stopped shaking. She started to believe once more that she might be able to carry out what she'd come to do, however absurd or unrealistic it might have seemed.

Marah pulled to within ten feet of Wahab. He cupped his hands together and made a low, whistling birdcall, and a moment later, Marah heard a similar call in the distance. She squeezed the barrel and stock of the machine gun so tightly that her knuckles blanched; her mouth grew dry, and her heart pounded in her throat. She soon spotted the clearing in the distance. Then she saw Flaco walk through the clearing. She spotted another machine gun leaning against a kamagong tree, which must've belonged to Mustafa. If they were all there, then it was likely that Eden was there, too, assuming that he was still alive.

Marah slipped her index finger through the trigger guard and raised the machine gun, then pointed it at the center of Wahab's back. If she could take out Wahab and

Flaco before they could fire upon her, she might have a chance against Mustafa. It was as good of an opportunity as she could've asked for, and she knew it might be her only opportunity as well.

She closed one eye and squinted through the sight. Her hands began trembling again, and Wahab's back swayed in and out of the crosshairs. Marah took in a slow breath, held it, and then leveled the machine gun before her. It suddenly seemed rock-steady in her hands, and the middle of Wahab's back remained squarely in the center of the crosshairs.

Now is the time, she thought to herself.

Before her finger could pull the trigger, though, she watched Eden emerge from one of the huts, holding a bottled water in his right hand.

CHAPTER TWENTY-FOUR

Marah spoke when she saw Eden, her words tumbling forth from her mouth like a cough.

"The fuck . . . ?"

Startled, Eden turned and looked in Marah's direction, and Flaco and Wahab turned as well. No one moved, and time seemed to stand still; even the jungle noise seemed to fade away and disappear.

After what felt like an eternity, Eden finally spoke.

"Baby — ?"

Wahab began to raise his M16, but Marah reflexively pointed her machine gun at him before he could.

"Drop it," she said, her heart hammering in her chest.

Wahab hesitated.

"I said drop it!" she shouted. "Now!"

Wahab slowly bent down and placed his machine gun on the ground before him.

"Thank God you're okay—"

Marah interrupted Eden.

"What the fuck's going on?" she said.

"I was about to ask you the same thing," he said, looking toward the forest beyond her.

"What?"

"Where's the longhaired guy?"

Marah hesitated, seized by a sudden panic. *Had she made a terrible mistake? Had her mother and stepfather actually come through with the money?*

"Marah?"

She continued to hesitate, torn and bewildered.

"Where is he?" said Eden.

The men looked toward Eden, and though no words were spoken, something seemed to pass between them, some vague sort of complicity. Marah noticed it, and Eden seemed to notice her noticing it as well.

"What was that?" she said, flabbergasted.

"What was what?"

He can't be involved in this, she thought to herself. *Or could he be?* She suddenly wasn't so sure; a hazy sense of suspicion and disbelief shoved aside Marah's initial feeling of shock.

"He just looked to you," she said.

"Don't be ridiculous," he said, taking a step toward Wahab's gun.

She turned the gun on him, a knee-jerk reaction.

"Don't move," she said.

"Come on," said Eden, laughing and continuing toward Wahab's gun. "Be serious—"

Marah shakily pointed the gun at his chest.

"I said don't move!" she shouted.

Eden froze, no longer smiling. "We're going home, baby," he said. "It's over."

She hesitated, wanting to believe him but becoming less and less sure. She searched his eyes for an answer, some sort of indication or reinforcement, but she couldn't find one.

"What were you doing in that hut?" she said.

"What are you talking about?" he said, taking another step toward her.

"Stay back!" she shouted, pointing the gun at his chest.

"Baby, you gotta think straight here—"

Eden continued to advance, and she fired at the ground before him, surprising even herself, the gun jumping in her hands.

"Jesus Christ!" he screamed. "What the fuck's the matter with you?"

Marah kept the machine gun pointed at Eden.

"I said stay back!" she said.

A hazy picture emerged in her mind, the puzzle pieces slowly coming together; Eden's recent and growing distance toward her, the adjustments to their finances in the previous months, the urgent need for the vacation, her ever-deepening depression clouding her judgment . . . it all started to make sense, a too-perfect sense. *Or was it the too-perfect sense of the insane?* she began to wonder, like the labyrinthine conspiracy theories of her dementia-addled grandmother, or the schizophrenic classmate of hers at NYU who thought aliens were trying to communicate to him through the subway trains. *Could Eden really have been involved?* she wondered. It somehow seemed unfathomable. *But what the hell was he doing inside the hut, and why were the men not watching him?* She went around and around in her mind, unable to come up with a logical explanation.

"Come on, Marah," said Eden. "Lower the gun."

A part of her wanted to, and for it to be over, but she continued to hesitate, unsure.

"You're not thinking straight, baby," he said, taking a small step toward her. "You know I'd never do anything to hurt you . . ."

As Eden slowly continued to approach her, the machine gun grew heavier and heavier in her grip. She found her resolve weakening, and she again searched his eyes for answers or clues, but there were none; they were hollow and empty, like the eyes of the stuffed sheep in Abu Tuan's trunk.

"Come on, let's go home—"

Before Eden could finish, Marah heard a sound in the jungle behind her. She turned and followed Eden's eye line toward the origin of the sound and saw Mustafa approaching, holding his bolo knife. *Eden must've seen him coming the whole time*, she thought to herself. *How could he have not?*

"Wait—"

Ignoring Eden, Marah fired the machine gun at Mustafa, the bullets punching into the ground at his feet, then his groin and torso, and then his neck. As Mustafa fell to the ground clutching his throat, blood spurting from his neck in a bright, red fan, Marah spun back around, and her eyes briefly met Eden's. The expression on his face— an odd, remorseless mixture of anger and surprise— chilled her to her core. Before she could react, Flaco dove for Wahab's machine gun.

"Don't do it!" she shouted. Ignoring her, Flaco grabbed it and fired at Marah, hitting her in the shoulder. She fired back and hit him in the chest and gut, then aimed at Wahab and pulled the trigger, but the gun came up empty, and Wahab bolted.

"Marah—!"

Before Eden could finish, Marah dropped the empty machine gun and fled into the jungle.

Marah ran through the wilderness, scrambling over rocks and fallen trees. She looked down at her wounded shoulder; it bled steadily from a nickel-sized wound, and she couldn't lift it more than a few inches. It felt like someone had stuck a hot poker through her. Eden shouted after her, following from a distance.

"Marah, wait!"

She grit her teeth, enraged, continuing on without looking back. She knew he must've been involved somehow. *But how, exactly?* she wondered. *And more importantly, why?* She couldn't figure it out, but the more she thought about it, the more enraged she became.

After losing her footing, she tumbled down a hill, coming down hard on her injured shoulder. She looked behind her and saw Eden cutting the distance between them.

"I just want to talk!" he said.

Marah struggled back to her feet and continued on. Before long, she approached a swamp choked with mangroves. She looked over her shoulder and saw Eden gaining, then looked back ahead at the dense tangle of foliage.

Eden shouted after her.

"Marah, please!"

Marah entered the swamp. She waded forward into the murky waters, past her shins, then her knees, and then up to her waist. She stopped when the water level reached her chest, then looked back and saw Eden entering the swamp about a hundred feet behind her.

"Marah!" he shouted.

Marah turned around and trudged onward, blotting out the sound of his voice. She couldn't bear to hear it anymore; it was like being in a nightmare, and what was happening now was even worse than the kidnapping itself. She paddled through a deep stretch of water. Then she resumed slogging through the muck. Spotting a copse of old mangroves, she changed direction, and when she reached the trees, she hid under a thick tangle of mangrove roots, crouching down so the water nearly reached her mouth.

She watched as Eden approached in the distance. As the adrenalin rush began to diminish, she felt a foggy sense of disbelief settling in. She heard the Radiohead lyric in her head again. *I'm not here*, she could hear Thom Yorke wailing. *This isn't happening.* A part of her still wanted to listen to Eden, despite all rational thought, but another, growing part of her told her not to listen and to stay away from him no matter what transpired.

She ducked down farther into the water as Eden continued to approach.

"Baby, please," he said.

She held her breath as Eden drew near.

"Just tell me what you want to do," he said. "All right? I'll do whatever you want."

She froze as he came within twenty feet of her, torn. A small part of her wanted to step forward and embrace him; he was still her husband, after all, the one who massaged her feet when they watched *Breaking Bad* and took her to a Massive Attack show in Japan for her thirty-third birthday. *But who was he, really?* she wondered. *What had he done, and what was he capable of doing?* She was no longer so sure.

Eden soon came so close to Marah that she could feel his movements through the water. She watched as he approached within fifteen feet of her, and then ten feet, and then five. For a moment, he hesitated, and she thought he saw her out of the corner of his eye. She closed her eyes and prepared for the worst, but after a few agonizing seconds, he continued past. She let out a deep, slow breath, relieved, then watched as Eden went forward through the swamp.

"Marah, please," he said.

She said nothing, remaining motionless. After he was about fifty feet away from her, Marah felt along the bottom of the swamp until she found a fist-sized rock. She hesitated for a moment, weighing it in her hand, considering it. Then she heaved it as far as she could. When it splashed down into the water, Eden pulled a pistol from his waistband and fired in its direction, blasting a mangrove to shreds. Once the water settled, he exploded, realizing it wasn't her.

"Fuck!"

Marah sank down again as deep as she could, hiding among the mangrove roots. Whatever doubt she'd had about his intentions all but evaporated; she felt heartbroken, but her racing thoughts finally began to slow down, and her breathing slowed as well. She watched as Eden continued to search the swamp, ejecting the spent clip from the pistol and slamming a full one in its place.

"You think you're so smart, don't you?" he shouted. "You always thought you were so much better than me!"

Marah glanced around at her surroundings for a way out. She spotted the edge of the swamp in the distance, about a hundred feet away. At the same time, Eden continued to search for Marah, checking behind each copse of trees and under each tangle of mangrove branches.

"God dammit, Marah, come out here, now!" he shouted.

After a moment, Marah started for the edge of the

swamp, going as slowly and keeping as low as possible. Eden looked for signs of her, for movements in the surface of the water or other signs of motion.

"Marah?"

Ignoring him, she continued toward the edge of the swamp. After a moment, Eden lowered the pistol.

"Baby, I'm sorry," he said, his voice taking on a radically different tone. "I didn't mean that . . ."

Marah advanced toward the edge of the swamp, ignoring him and staying as low to the water as possible. Behind her, Eden noticed some ripples on the surface of the water swelling toward him. He changed direction, heading back toward the swamp edge.

"It wasn't supposed to happen like this," he said. "I was gonna pay your parents back. I was gonna help these guys, too. No one was supposed to get hurt."

Marah continued toward the edge of the swamp. Behind her, Eden advanced, heading toward the origin of the water's disturbance. After a moment, he hung the pistol from a tree branch.

"Look, I'm putting down the gun, okay?" he said. "See? I just want to talk, that's all."

Marah picked up her speed at the edge of the swamp as it shallowed out, wading through the muck. Behind her, Eden spun around when he heard the splashing and saw Marah leaving the swamp.

"Marah . . . ?"

She didn't stop. He went back for the pistol and took it down from the branch, then took aim and fired in her direction. She ducked the bullets as they tore through the leaves and trees around her, continuing on her way. Eden left the swamp and bolted after Marah, the pistol raised.

"Marah!" he shouted, enraged.

She picked up the stream and ran back in the direction of the clearing, pure instinct and unencumbered by thought. She continued on without stopping, the branches whipping her torso and limbs. Eden ran through the jungle in pursuit of her, hurtling fallen logs and swatting vines and branches out of his way. Before long, she approached the clearing.

"Marah, come on!" shouted Eden.

She went over to Mustafa's body and took his bolo knife. Then, as Eden approached the clearing, she ducked back into the jungle. She watched from behind a copse of kamagong trees as Eden calmly walked through the clearing, looking for her. Then she glanced around, spotting a tangle of boxthorn bushes nearby.

"Look, we can do this together, or I can do it alone," he said. "It's your call."

Marah hesitated for a moment as Eden continued to search the camp. Once he seemed far enough away from her, she slowly took off her shirt and hung it from the boxthorns.

"Come on, Marah," he said. "It doesn't have to be this way."

Eden wandered the camp, checking the huts and beginning to look along the tree line. Marah hid behind a rubber tree and watched as Eden checked the ground for her footprints. After a moment, Eden spotted Marah's shirt in the tangle of boxthorns. She watched as he crept toward the jungle, holding the pistol at his side. Her heart began to hammer in her chest, and she took a long, deep breath, holding it in for a few seconds before slowly letting it back out.

As Eden approached the empty shirt, Marah emerged from the stand of trees, gripping the bolo knife. Hearing something behind him, Eden started to turn around, but before he could raise the pistol, Marah swung the bolo knife, hacking down through his collarbone. He dropped the pistol, groaning in pain.

"Bitch!" he said, eyes aflame with rage.

Eden tackled Marah, and they hit the ground in a heap, where they struggled for control of the knife. Arterial blood gushed from Eden's wound, soaking their clothing and painting the earth red. Unable to pry the knife free, Eden grabbed Marah's wrist and smashed it against the ground until the knife came loose. Using his good arm, he reached across his body for the knife, but just before he could get it, Marah managed to kick it away. Eden grabbed Marah's throat with his free hand and began to choke her.

"I'll kill you!" he shouted.

He tightened his grip, and she began to pass out. Things started to go black. She could hear the loud, angry voice in her head saying, *I told you so,* but before it could say more, the calm, steady voice spoke, saying, *Don't give up*, louder and louder. She pried at his fingers until she was able to get some air, and then she pried at them some more until she managed to peel one of them away. Then she struggled it up to her mouth, where she bit down on it as hard as she could, tasting his salty blood and crunching against the knucklebone. He screamed in pain. She kneed him in the groin and managed to scramble out from underneath him, gasping for air. Then she struggled to her feet, and he lunged for her ankle with his bleeding hand, but she easily kicked it away.

"Wait," he said, reaching again for her leg.

He grabbed her by the ankle and she fell to the ground, landing hard on her side. As he started to pull her back toward him, she grabbed the pistol, then turned over and fired at him. The first shot missed Eden, but the second hit him in the chest, and he let go of her ankle.

She fired again and again at Eden until the gun was empty and he finally stopped moving.

CHAPTER TWENTY-FIVE

Marah dropped the pistol and staggered away. She again felt the urge to throw up, and after a moment, she doubled over and vomited onto the ground. As soon as she was finished, she wiped her mouth with the back of her hand, then went back over and looked at Eden. She hardly recognized him, and it wasn't just the injuries he'd sustained, either; beneath all the blood and dirt, his face looked like a mask, malleable and blank. *Who were you?* she wondered, both dumbfounded and shocked. *And how could I have been so blind?* She slowly shook her head, completely at a loss for words.

After a long moment, she leaned down and touched the side of his neck with her trembling fingers, checking for his pulse. Feeling his soft, familiar stubble, which had grazed her cheeks so many countless times, a sob rose in her throat, but she swallowed it and stifled the urge to cry. She moved away from him and tried the cell phone again, but there was still no reception. She then approached Mustafa's body, knelt down, and checked his pockets for a cell, but there wasn't one. She checked Flaco's pockets as well, but he didn't have a cell, either. He looked even younger in death, like a choirboy, and another sob rose in her throat. Marah choked back the urge to cry, and she picked up Flaco's machine gun. There was no time for emotion; if she wanted to survive, she knew she needed to go, now, and not to think about it or look back.

She searched the camp, but the huts were empty, and the other machine gun was nowhere to be found; perhaps Wahab had taken it. After a moment, she heard the sound of a branch bending somewhere in the jungle nearby. She raised the machine gun and spun around, only to see a bird taking flight from its perch. Feeling vulnerable and out in the open, Marah left the camp and reentered the jungle.

She fought her way through a dense stretch of tangled shrubs, jagged rocks, and large, woody vines that flayed her bare torso and thighs. She trudged up and down a series of hills, looking for the thin stream she'd crossed on her way in from the beach. More time passed than she remembered the trip from the beach to the camp taking, but she still didn't find the stream. She continued onward, assuming it was somewhere nearby.

She soon reached another rise. An impassable stretch of jagged boulders and undergrowth lay before her. She looked back over her shoulder, but she didn't recognize anything. She looked ahead and to her right and left; nothing looked familiar.

She closed her eyes and listened for the sound of the ocean, but all she could hear was the incessant buzzing of the insects.

The full moon shone above the island, casting a milky net over the darkness of the jungle. Marah crossed a swampy plain under the light of the moon, slipping and sliding her way through the mud. She held the machine gun before her, her finger hovering over the trigger. Her wounded shoulder throbbed and continued to bleed; at one point, she twisted her ankle in the muck, and within seconds, it swelled to the size of an orange, ablaze with sharp pain. There was nothing she could do, though, so she struggled onward, gritting her teeth every time she stepped down on it.

After fighting through a dense stretch of tangled shrubs, Marah trudged up and down a series of hills. She didn't come to the stream she'd crossed on her way in, but she continued on, assuming she'd eventually find it. She tried to stay present and focused, but she couldn't stop thinking about Eden. Scores of questions flooded her mind, but they were all more or less variations of the same simple one: *Why?*

Marah soon passed through another dense stretch of undergrowth, and then she traversed another series of low hills. Again, she found no stream, and even in the near-darkness, she could see that she was in an area that looked completely unfamiliar to her. She felt the urge to lie down and rest, but knowing that she might never get back up, she carried on. Before long, she reached another rise, and after cresting it, the jungle sloped off before her to both sides.

Marah looked to her right and then to her left. After another moment, she set off down the right side of the slope, slipping and sliding her way through the decaying leaves.

The nocturnal sounds of the mosquitos and the flapping moths soon gave way to the music of the frogs, morning birds, and other harbingers of dawn. The sun was still just a faint rumor on the horizon that couldn't be seen through the thick canopy of trees, but hints of its coming warmth and light began to slowly make their way down toward the jungle floor.

Marah crossed a swampy plain in a half-asleep, half-awake daze. Blood continued to seep from the bullet wound on her shoulder, which ached like it'd been hit with a baseball bat. After crossing the plain, she entered yet another stretch of thick jungle. She'd already given up on her fantasies of finding a village or even civilization at all and now hoped that she would merely survive somehow, and not end up becoming a rotting corpse in the middle of some nameless jungle.

The sun rose as Marah crossed another swampy plain, painting the sky in gaudy hues of purple and orange. It slowly burned away the shroud of mist that had blanketed the jungle at night, revealing the distinct outlines of the thick forest all around her. Marah looked back behind her and saw the top of the sun pushing above the horizon. It was an even more beautiful sight out in the open, unhindered by the canopy of trees; the bright, dreamy colors reminded her of the rainbow sherbet she and her sister had gorged themselves on as children. It was hard to enjoy, though, knowing that she was lost in the jungle and possibly being hunted at that moment, so she looked ahead and trudged onward.

All around her, the birds were taking flight from their nests, wailing and crying as they went about their morning work. The heat began to ratchet up again like a warming sauna. After a while, Marah heard a faint whispering in the distance. She turned and craned her neck to listen; at first, all she could hear were distant birds and the buzz of the insects, but after a moment, she was able to pick out a sound from the rest of the noise. It sounded soft and soothing, like a mother hushing a child to sleep.

Marah started in the direction of the origin of the sound. Before long, she broke into a run, despite the throbbing pain of her injured ankle. She soon emerged from the jungle and onto the beachhead, where she ran down to the shore. Then she dropped the machine gun and plunged into the ocean without breaking stride.

She dove underneath an approaching wave, taking in a mouthful of water and swallowing it despite the overpowering taste of salt. Then she dove underneath the next wave, and the next. For a brief moment, she forgot who she was and where she was and what had happened, immensely relieved to be in the water and out of the jungle. Then she remembered that Wahab was still out there, and she turned and looked inland.

Every shadow she saw was menacing, and she imagined someone hiding behind every tree.

The midday sun beat down upon the island. Heat waves

rose shimmering from the hot sand, and the coastal birds sought refuge in the jungle.

Marah approached the part of the coastline where they'd originally entered the jungle. The boat was nowhere to be seen, the ocean a blank canvas. She continued to trudge her way up the coast, eventually approaching a wide berm studded with sand dunes. As she got closer to the dunes, she began to see that the sand was all churned up; at first, it looked like there'd been a volleyball game there, but the closer she got, the more the markings looked like footprints and drag marks. She grew sick to her stomach, wondering who or what might have left the marks. Before long, she spotted a pair of egrets furiously digging through the churned-up sand. A large frigate bird hopped over and joined in, jabbing its long, hooked bill into the ground. After a moment, the frigate bird's open bill reemerged, holding what looked like a ping-pong ball. The bird then swallowed the object whole before jabbing its bill back into the sand.

Marah hurried over to the dunes, where she dropped to her hands and knees and began to dig through the sand. Within seconds, she found a clutch of turtle eggs. She picked up one and studied it for a moment, then peeled open its rubbery shell and took a whiff. It smelled like semen, musty and ammoniac, but she'd never been hungrier in her life.

Marah pinched her nose and threw back the egg like an oyster. After choking it down, she peeled open another egg and sucked it down, and then another.

She gorged herself, gagging, until she could eat no more.

A scattering of clouds passed over the island, thin as pulled cotton. They diminished the sun for a while, but the respite was short-lived; the winds grew in the east, soon pushing them out to sea.

Marah stumbled onward, exhausted. She mumbled the Dickinson poem under her breath, again and again, her parched voice little more than a whisper.

She looked down at the ground and saw a set of tracks that looked just like hers. Then she looked out toward the ocean. There wasn't a single light or landmass anywhere on the horizon. The loud, angry voice returned to her thoughts, telling her in a mocking tone that it served her right, and that she should begin preparing for her end. She pushed it from her thoughts and continued on, and before long, the calm, steady voice reappeared, blotting it out. *Keep going,* it said, over and over again like a mantra. *Just keep going.* She soon realized that she was saying the words out loud herself as well, in unison with the voice in her head.

She trudged onward. After a while, she heard voices in the distance. *Am I dreaming?* she wondered. *Or are they real?* She glanced around, looking for their origin. Then, remembering that Wahab was still out there, she scanned her surroundings, looking for cover. She spotted some sand dunes in the distance, up the coast, and ran toward them, hiding behind a tangle of dry beach grass.

Marah looked out toward the water. She soon saw a thin wooden boat approaching, carrying four men. *Are they Zamboangueño, or Moro, or Bajau?* she wondered. *Are they pirates or fishermen?* She couldn't tell; there was no clear indication either way.

She hesitated, torn. Then she watched one of the men reach into the hull of the boat. She raised the machine gun, bracing herself. Then the man pulled up a tattered fishing net, which he cast out over the sun-dappled water.

Go, said the calm, steady voice in her head. The loud, angry voice reappeared, telling her to stay where she was, and that it was a trap. But the calm, steady voice persisted, growing louder and louder in volume with each iteration. *Go,* it urged her. *Now.*

After a moment, Marah dropped the machine gun and stumbled down toward the water. She shouted, but her throat was so dry that hardly more than a whisper emerged.

"Help me," she said.

The men didn't hear her. She tried again, louder, waving her arms.

"Please," she said. "Help."

Again, they didn't hear her. She shouted as loud as she could, a raspy croak finally emerging from her throat.

"Help!"

The fishermen finally looked up at her, startled to see a Westerner. They took in their net and paddled in to meet her, and when they neared the coastline, two of the men jumped out of the boat and splashed toward her, chattering excitedly in Bajau.

"American," she said. "I'm an American . . . *Amerikano* . . . I was taken hostage . . ."

The fishermen didn't seem to understand her, and she didn't understand them, either, but one of them understood the situation enough to offer her a plastic jug of water.

"Thank you," she said, gulping it down as they helped her into their boat. She drank more, choking on it, letting it splash down her chin and chest. Then she looked back as the men slowly turned the boat around and began to head away from the island, and she saw vague shapes in the dark jungle, emerging like images in a Rorschach test. There were crows, oil spills, and animal hides; there were huge, blooming flowers, butterflies, and flowing robes. And there were faces; at first, she saw Eden's face, and then her own, as if in the reflection of a mirror, and then a child's, and finally, a blank mask. Something hit her like a wave—a sudden surge of grief, terror, pain, and frustration, all at the same time. She started to laugh, as if out of nowhere, and it was a shock to her. Then the laughter turned to tears. She tried to hold it back, but she couldn't; there was just too much.

She finally allowed it all to come out, sobbing uncontrollably as the island faded into the distance.

CHAPTER TWENTY-SIX
NEW YORK CITY – SIX WEEKS LATER

Marah woke with a start, soaked with sweat. A new cell phone rang on the other side of the room, next to the cardboard box it had come in. She glanced around, disoriented for a moment before remembering that she was in her new apartment on the Lower East Side. There were a few cardboard boxes stacked against one wall, full of clothes and essentials, but other than that, the room was empty.

She got out of bed and approached the ringing cell. After finishing the inquiries in Malaysia—first with the Malaysian officials, and then with the US and Chinese officials as well as Eden's employers, from whom she'd learned about Eden's vastly overextended credit as well as the significant sum of money that he'd stolen from the firm — she promptly returned to Shanghai and packed her things on her own, despite numerous offers of help from family and friends. Her stepfather and mother had even purchased plane tickets to fly over, but she told them that she didn't want them to come. Everyone had suggested she take some time off before deciding what to do, but she'd ignored them all, flying immediately to New York and taking the first apartment that she could find before applying for teaching jobs at a number of private schools. She wanted to move on and to move forward rather than to dwell on what had occurred.

Marah's eyes stopped when she passed a mirror. It took a second to register that she was looking at her own reflection and not someone else's; with her lightened, shortened hairstyle and the way that her broken nose had asymmetrically healed, she almost didn't recognize herself. But that was the whole point; after Semporna, she'd wanted a fresh start, and she'd done everything that she could've to make that happen.

She continued on and picked up the ringing cell.

"Marah Matthews," she said, using her maiden name, which she'd been doing since her return to America.

A nasally voice spoke on the other end of the line.

"Hi, Marah, it's Libbie Stolberg, from the Dalton

School."

Before the conversation could continue, an intense feeling of nausea overcame Marah. She clutched her stomach.

"Sorry, can I call you back?" she said, stifling the urge to vomit.

Without waiting for a reply, Marah hung up the phone and ducked into the bathroom. Once inside it, she dropped to her hands and knees and promptly threw up into the toilet.

Taxicabs and ambulances came and went from the shoebox-shaped NewYork-Presbyterian Hospital. The midday sun crashed against the building's glass façade, reflecting back across lower Manhattan.

Marah sat inside a gynecologist's office, chewing a ragged fingernail. She looked to the diplomas on the wall. Then she glanced out the window toward the street below. Taxis and mopeds battled for position in the heavy traffic, while tourists and locals teemed along the narrow sidewalks, jockeying for space.

She checked the time on her cell phone. It was already 12:49, just ten minutes until the interview she'd arranged at the Chapin School, which was all the way uptown on the East Side. She started to write an email asking to postpone the interview when the door to the office opened. A short, bespectacled Asian woman in her late fifties entered the room, startling Marah.

"Sorry to keep you waiting," said the woman, surprising Marah with her harsh Bronx accent as she closed the door behind her.

"That's okay," said Marah.

The doctor sat down behind the desk.

"So," she said, looking at Marah's file through her thick glasses. "You know why you're here, don't you?"

Marah shook her head, but when the doctor grinned, it suddenly dawned on her.

Of course, Marah thought to herself, flabbergasted. *How could I not have known?*

Marah had three more interviews that week, at the Spence School, Riverdale, and Horace Mann. Every morning, she went for a long run along the river, and in the afternoons, she went shopping for clothes and furnishings for her apartment.

On Friday morning, she went to the Family Planning Clinic at NewYork-Presbyterian. Her appointment was at 9:30, but she got there at 8:15, and she read two issues of *Time* magazine while waiting for her name to be called. As soon as it finally was, a nurse led her to a private room and gave her a gown to change into, and while she did, she saw her reflection in a mirror and looked down at her midsection, wondering what the fetus inside her looked like. *Does it have a face yet? Does it have fingernails, or hair? Does it look like him, or like me . . . or like neither, and just like itself?*

Growing uncomfortable, Marah pushed the thoughts from her mind and finished putting on the gown. *I can't keep it,* she thought to herself. *It'd have no father, and I can't imagine looking at a child that looks like Eden for the rest of my life.* Then she heard another, smaller voice in her thoughts. *But what if this is the only chance you'll ever have? And what would it really have to do with Eden, anyway? Wasn't it – or more appropriately, he or she – his or her own being?*

After a moment, someone knocked at the door, startling her. "Ms. Matthews?"

"Come in," said Marah.

A young nurse entered the room. Though she was probably in her late twenties, she looked like a teenager.

"I'm going to give you a quick checkup before the procedure," said the nurse. "Will there be a support person for you today?"

Marah shook her head; her mother would've come into the city in a heartbeat, and her college roommate, Geraldine, who worked at NASDAQ, would've gladly taken the day off if asked, but Marah hadn't told anyone, and she'd scheduled the first available appointment they'd had. The nurse put a cuff over Marah's upper arm and measured Marah's blood pressure, noting it in a file, then checked Marah's pulse.

"I'm going to give you something that will help with the discomfort, okay?" said the nurse.

Marah nodded. The nurse began preparing an IV line, and Marah looked out the window at the street below. She felt a sharp prick as the nurse pushed the IV needle into her arm, and a moment later, the nurse administered a shot. A soft, warm feeling soon began to creep up Marah's neck and radiate out from her center.

"Are you feeling all right, Ms. Matthews?" asked the nurse.

Marah nodded.

"The doctor will be right in," said the nurse.

Marah nodded again and looked back out the window, watching the morning traffic below. A part of her felt nervous, and another part of her felt relief, yet something still nagged at her. *Was it guilt?* she wondered. *Or doubt?* She weighed her options again, and no matter how she looked at the situation, any other solution didn't make sense, logistically, financially, intellectually, or, perhaps most importantly, emotionally.

After a long moment, the door opened, and the doctor entered the room. "Are we ready?" she asked.

"Yes, Dr. Chin," said the nurse.

The doctor and nurse prepared for the procedure, putting on gloves, adjusting lights, and opening packages of sterilized equipment. As soon as she was finished, the doctor turned to the nurse.

"Let's begin," she said.

The nurse nodded. Marah watched them as they went about their preparations, her heartbeat quickening in her chest. The pain medication gently pulled her away from the scene, urging her to go elsewhere, and to let go. But her feelings of apprehension remained, slowly and steadily building in strength like an approaching wave.

Just as they were about to start the procedure, Marah struggled upright in bed, fighting against the numbing effects of the pain medication. She covered her crotch with her hand and opened her mouth to speak.

"Wait," she said.

ACKNOWLEDGEMENTS

I'm indebted to the editorial guidance of Laura Mae Isaacman, Anna Hogarty, Grace Ross, DeAndra Lupu, and Ryan Quinn. Thanks also to Rob Tregenza, Darrell Fusaro, my family, friends, colleagues, and students, and last but certainly not least, to Lauren, Amalie, and Anfinn, for each and every day.

ABOUT THE AUTHOR

Kirk Kjeldsen received an MFA from USC and is currently an assistant professor in the cinema program at VCU's School of the Arts. His first novel, *Tomorrow City*, was named one of the ten best books of 2013 by the *New Jersey Star-Ledger*. He also adapted the poetry of Tarjei Vesaas into the feature film *Gavagai*, directed by Rob Tregenza. He lives in Germany with his wife and two children.

9 780998 465739